what begins with bird

what begins with bird

by Noy Holland

FC2

NORMAL/TALLAHASSEE

Published by FC2 with support provided by Florida State University,
the Publications Unit of the Department of English at Illinois State
University, and the Florida Arts Council of the Florida Division of
Cultural Affairs

Address all inquiries to: Fiction Collective Two, Florida State University,
c/o English Department, Tallahassee, FL 32306-1580

ISBN: Paper, 1-57366-125-2

Library of Congress Cataloging-in-Publication Data
Holland, Noy, 1960-
  What begins with bird / by Noy Holland.— 1st ed.
     p. cm.
  ISBN 1-57366-125-2 (pbk.)
  1. United States—Social life and customs—Fiction. I. Title.
  PS3558.O3486W47 2005
  813'.54—dc22
                                        2005020390

Cover Design: Lou Robinson
Book Design: Tara Reeser

Produced and printed in the United States of America
Printed on recycled paper with soy ink

acknowledgements

I am grateful, as ever, to Will Eno and Gordon Lish—fierce readers and dear friends. Thank you, Dara. Also Lisa. I thank Francesco Clemente, the good Dick B., and—for his eye and ear—Ralph Berry. Thank you, Melissa Kathleen, for the courage of your example. I thank, with everything in me, my children—Benjamin Reno, and Phoebe Louise. May you prosper!

acknowledgements

The author gratefully acknowledges the National Endowment for the Arts, the Massachusetts Cultural Council, and the MacDowell Colony, for their generous support during the writing of this book.

"Rooster Pollard Cricket Goose" and a portion of "What Begins with Bird" originally appeared in *Conjunctions*; "Coquina" in *The American Voice*; "Fairway" in *Black Warrior Review*; "Time for the Flat-headed Man" in *Open City*; "Someone is always Missing" in *Glimmer Train*.

for Sam

contents

what begins with bird

I start the bulbs in the window the day she flies in from Mississippi. I stand them up in bowls of the gravel that I scraped from the driveway with a spoon—hours ago, when the ground still showed. Now the yard is a blank of snow. The crocuses are buried and broken.

The bulbs have gone spongy or peeling and split from sitting in paper sacks too long. I should have planted them in October, picked a hole in the pebbly ground. But back then I had things to do yet, things I could do, and I can't now. So I force hyacinth on the sill.

I sit among the brocade chairs and wait for the smallest changes: his lazy eye to open, a sound at the name in my mouth. We have named the boy after the city we succumbed to marriage in, in a storm as freaky as this one: wind from the north for Easter, our sky a pink velour. Our trees are as black as shadows of trees, pressed flat in this light and moaning.

Reno, Reno, Reno—without thinking, when we thought of his name, what a trial they are, those r's. *Weno*, we know. But we didn't know it then.

My sister will call the boy something else, no doubt, as soon as she has seen him, not sweetpea, nor pumpkin (I do), but by her weekly sweetheart's name, or somebody lost or dead. They die off early, turn up their toes in babbling sleep, down where my sister lives. She will arrive with photographs, mangled faces, folded into her pockets.

Or it could be the snow has stopped her, turned her back for home. We call it that, all of us: *home.* It is a family habit, this turning away, a lie we began her lifetime ago, gathered over her, immobile: a lump, for months, in her crib.

My sister lives in an institution. The place is built in the dusky bottomland of the Mississippi River, among stands of tri-fling hardwoods overrun by the south's Great Vine; even in winter the trees bow their heads to that gray roving appetite, a great hunger—acres consumed by the pestilence of kudzu.

Nothing grows as quickly here. The ivy is slow and civil. Our trees bend their heads for hours, a week, then toss off their burdens of snow. This can't last. A day of melt and the goose will be back to jab at the grassy patches.

Only the rabbit, in the surprise of cold, keeps to her routine: brazen creature, fixed as stone at the foot of the leaky birdbath. Frost has split the concrete bowl, parted the fluted column. These rotten New England winters. But everything else is calm: our one raccoon, the fat goose in our yard most mornings.

I tap at the glass. Not a flutter. Even the rabbit won't scare. She will keep to her place at the birdbath while night comes and day again, waiting—who can say for what? Instructions, I suppose, a murmur, a nudge, from her sack of eggs.

Small as he is, my boy trumpets, stiffens his back a little. These are *my* instructions. But there is nothing I know to do for him, nothing to do but cluck and drift and wait here for my sister. We pass such liquid, unmoored days—no sleep—with only outside the seeping beech, the rising snow to mark time by.

Love, love. I want nothing.

My boy draws up again inside me, nights, small body rocked shut, sweet thrill—to feel him pitch and tumble. The sea at night is yellow cream, a tongue from the waking shore.

Too soon—to be asked to speak, to rise and walk. They are slow, my tribe, by habit, to come (it is a birth, after all, not a funeral)—but even so this is too soon for me. I am still jerking awake at night and dressing for the hospital: the chalky, sudden sky, the gray road, salted, gritty, slush hissing from our wheels.

Still bleeding, the stuff dropping from me in great gobs.

I say none of this. What use? We are found out. There is no saying no to my sister. I hear her grinding her teeth over the phone, heels dug in, and her father, ours, our father has bought her the ticket to come. So we ready. I start the bulbs in the window—something more to watch for; I buy wrapped chocolate eggs. My turn—it has been decided, and there is no getting loose from my father either, even from afar.

He calls ahead to say to me, "They say she's been funny lately."

"Funny?"

"I don't know."

We move on to weather because this is also our habit; I am given the nationwide report before he asks about my son.

"Our Mr. Sun," I say, when he has embellished the heat in the Middle West with stories of rotting bodies, the elderly done in by stroke in the tenements of Chicago. This is when he seems to remember—that he ought to ask, to have already asked. We are both quiet, quietly breathing, and then my father plunges ahead.

"So how's the baby? Baby okay?" he says.

"Yes, yes—" he must be, though I wake him as so many mothers do to be certain he is still breathing. He grins in his sleep—these are dreams, I say—and startles. An arm flaps up. The lid of one eye heaves open.

Dear lump. I could round his pointy head, work the flat patch where he sleeps on it, the notched resilient plates, the bone still spongy as the bulbs I found to force in the gloom this morning. But I don't; it won't last; I leave him be.

I leave the plastic band on his wrist where Nurse Jane wrote my name—how strange, that you cannot at first even pick out your own from all the other babies. Mine has eleven dimples—dimples instead of knuckles and one on each side of his nose; in the fat of his leg is a pucker the color of pencil lead, a stitch drawn deep and tightly and tied off at the bone.

I knew him in the dark this way. I felt for the stitch in the dark of my room where the big windows looked at the Merrimack, the viscid fenced canal; I watched school children pasting up paper eggs and tousling in the hall and, once, one boy swung his lace-ups up to catch in the branch of a tree. They dropped, and the other boys spat and hooted. I kept it dark inside in my room for him so that when they brought him to me I knew him by his smell. He smelled of lanolin, clean and old and animal and bitter to me then and now and I knew him then as I do now by the feel of the stitch in his leg, not a stitch, nothing that will heal.

There is this, and the plastic band I will leave on his wrist until Sister has come and gone, my name, we had not named him yet, and there are too the ways in me to say as I do *mine:*

The cut in me, seeping still, the grinning stapled mouth: proof that he has been here, proof that he is gone. Here is where they found him, red and bawling, lifted him plumply out.

My belly-skin a lizard's, shrunk to shimmering and scale.

And here—this dimming streak, gray as ash, that marks me thatch to sternum; this line drawn through my navel that darkened as we grew. We grew, we grew.

I would have carried him in me for years.

And yet here in my face is the vessel I burst trying to push him out. Too late—by then he had already outgrown me, grown into me, a leggy, dogged stalk of boy left to bolt to seed. He left in my forehead the fine mesh of roots that living things send out, the paths, the swerving abruptions of blood, the friable clump in the floor of a pot, as though I had needed first, to birth him, to tear him from my brain.

I do not try to hide it. I obscure no proof, no possible claim.

I am claimed in the old animal way—the tails of my shirts, my thick brassieres, hair and neck and cupping ear: give him air and the spigot is on. All's well. All the lights green for Reno, his penis a plump blue cone. I roll it in its sheath between my fingers, gap the bleedy pinprick he pisses on me through.

And if he pisses on Sister? She will skrauk like a crow and giggle, wince, and I will be near, watching over, looking out for her as I used to do, as I look out for snow that slides from a roof, and listen—for the strained-rope sound a branch will make before it tears from the head of a tree. Who could trust her?

I am watchful these new days anyway of anything that moves—small dogs, a fat goose, his own father.

And my sister is always moving, even when she means to sit, or we are, one of us, the rest of us since Mother, we are moving her around. Giving her instructions, keeping her out of the way.

She has a way of making her absence felt. You know better— you should not have let her go. But she is bored, nervous, sullen. She grows weary, quickly, of family, needs somebody new to love. She comes to you for a visit and next you know she has disappeared. It is a monsoon, or a blizzard; you have made your nest in the desert, earthquakes coming, or it is the year of the romance of slums. Scarcely matters. She will wander out into anything, take up with anyone, drift off with the nearest miscreant to look at his tattoos.

I am like her in this; I move away. Even an infant finds safety in motion.

I never settled for years long enough for my father to send her to me, to track me down with news. But he is a good tracker: give him time, he finds you, elated some: some twister gouged the riverbanks, floods in Tennessee. The dying bees all summer. All preamble, priming, the news delivered first that you can do nothing about. And then, *your sister*—calling her not by name, of course, but by title, binding clause. The slippery possessive. *Your sister. My daughter.* Under what condition does he call her that—her, I think, or me?

It used to be we tracked down a new place for her every few months, every year. Our father's house, the YMCA—disastrous. Some school near here in Boston that packed her off in a blink to the loony bin. A problem of climate, my father decided. These dreary New England winters. The desert was next, saguaros and sun, the sobriety of a mineral landscape. She burned down her apartment, dropped a lighted cigarette into a heap of dirty laundry. That was Phoenix, and she was pregnant, a condition nobody noticed until she was six months along. Then the family engaged, oh, oh—moved in for the crisis.

We are a family that loves a good crisis. Birth control? I'd have thought that you… None of us had bothered.

Our father found me, enlisted me; it was a time in my life he could find me, when he could *call in the troops*, as he said. He flew me out to Phoenix first to see if I could persuade her. My father knew of a clinic not far from him, convenient to him, in Atlanta. I was to fly her back over the country to him, to the house we left our boxes in, in the town we had once called home. He had his Triptiks in order. He had his prim new wife. He had mapped out places to show to his wife on the drive to the clinic in Atlanta.

On the flight west I had my soothing, brief heroic moment, or the thought of one, the big idea. Nothing lasts with me. But for a moment I thought I would take her in, be her good big sister— quick, quick, before Daddy comes. Six months. By then a baby is swallowing; it is opening and closing its eyes. It had begun to hear, to know her voice. It must have turned toward the light as mine did, as I felt him face the sun.

Any light, even this gray gloaming, my boy turns his head to see, though he still sees nearly nothing, no distance, mostly only we keepers, mostly only me.

She stays put now, my sister; the grounds are fenced and gated.

Another bellow—raspy and prolonged. I am beginning to know the difference—between hunger, say, and fear. I lift him to me. I am dripping milk. His mouth opens quick as a bird's.

My breasts are stiff, prickly, lumped. He is rooting, and then uprooting me—that's what it feels like. I feel the tug in the wing of my shoulder and in the ball and socket; he is drawing my ribs together, cinching the narrowing slots; he is dragging silt from my bones.

All's well. Night soon. Above us, the snow is ticking down. No distance. No lapsed horizon bleeding pink beyond the flattened trees.

Little raccoon, funny monkey. He drinks and drinks and dozes. Yawns, and the trough in his wrinkled palate shows, slender and deep for sucking. A blister fills on his lip again, the skin of his first mouth already shed, the pale strips frayed and loosened.

Our rabbit flickers her ear. A squirrel drops out of the ging-ko tree at the far gray rim of our yard. Everything in its place; a place for everything. A patch of dirt for the sickly elm, a barn for broken china, rake and nail and rusting plow, a crib he will soon grow into.

It is all always too soon for me, the crib in the wings, the coming melt, the year's slow resurrection. The steadfast family wagon—my sister fetched from the airport—yawing into the drive.

I lay the boy down in his wicker tub and wheel him away from the door, from the surge of cold when it opens and damp and the squalling of crows in the heads of the trees and the plows groaning out on the highway.

Ready? I think. *Ready?* Because it has already begun.

My sister is out of the car and running at us before George even opens his door, all teeth and arms and flagging hair, a sidelong lurch and stutter. It is motion, the infant's comfort, mine, which gives her away. When she stops in the doorway and holds out her hands, waiting for me to come to her, nothing seems so wrong. She is pretty, and she has mastered the phony, square-bottomed smile taught in better homes: clean gums, corrected rows of teeth.

I move to her to see what I already know, cannot—would not—keep from seeing: the tremor, the scars, her bitten lip, the puddles of shadow around her eyes.

She stamps the snow from her sandals, standing wobbling in the doorway, the cold still streaming in. She hugs me, knocks against my chest. It always feels to me that her heart runs rough, won't idle, wants to race and quit; it is worse every time I see her and tells more clearly what is to come. They come mildly even now to me: days I cannot stop shaking. Another family habit—inherited, her tremor, worse with age (what isn't?) among the women in our tribe.

She keeps holding me so I stand there, stroking her hair, feeling her shudder against me. The first hour or two is an act with us, as with the early weeks of love. Easy enough, early on, to be sweeter than you are, to keep your few good secrets. But give a girl time, weather, meals. Quit closing the shithouse door. Pretty soon, this is me, I am chewing my tongue just to sit in the kitchen and listen to her, to the squalor of her feeding.

Those shoes—skinny, strappy things—and the snow some inches deep by now and she has left our George out in it, please, to gather up her bags. "It's like Cream of Wheat," she says, too loudly, "mercy."

It is a game they two have been playing, I guess, passing the time from the airport.

"It's like walking through frozen beer—" that is George's, and he laughs, and water pools as he walks in his footsteps and slops across the porch. He tips his hat.

"Hello, rabbit." He kisses me. "Hello, mother. Made it."

The trick must be in knowing who to be afraid of, what.

Our spotted dog, pent up, neglected, pokes her nose around the corner, suffers a paroxysm of joy—somebody fresh to love.

"So how is it in Mississippi?" I ask.

"Nice. Very nice. Flowers and such. But *cold* at night. Mercy."

She shakes the wet from her head, teasing, at the dog who quivers and blinks at her feet. "So where is he? Where's that baby?" She throws her hair back. "C'mere, young'n. Come here."

Somebody fresh to love; somebody new to harvest.

I am watchful, and sick in my heart to see the boy calmed in his own father's arms. What use, to see it coming? Bed down one yellow afternoon when the tide is in your favor and you begin the long moving away. Months pass; joints soften, slip; veins give, the blood in you doubles and quickens.

And yet this was not the feel of it—not of quickening, not to me, but of paths begun to silt and pinch, to slow, and, slowing, close. My neck swelled; my lungs rode up.

I fell into myself calmly, besotted and sufficient.

I was sufficient and am no longer, will not be again. Any mother knows.

The body remembers, seems to insist—there was something it meant to do—to lose him, to birth him. To finish what it had begun.

I wake, and find the boy beside me in the ripening bed, my bed. I keep him near me, the nightlight on, the barn beyond the window gone tossing out to sea. I drag the sheets back. His eyes are sprung open. His skin is twisted on him, rubbery and slick. He is not mine, is not the real baby. There is one yet still to be born.

There is everything still to go through again—my belly a stained translucence, the doctors in their starched blues.

Stupid, I know, to think it, want it. But even now, these weeks gone past, the small hard snaps of milk in his chest—witch's milk—dissolved; his lazy eye, the slackened lid, begun to draw up and quicken, so soon: I would go through it all all over again: the idiot howling, blood sliding from me in hot strings. Hours of this and then nothing, the needle pressed into the spine. The limp pale drape someone hung at my chest to keep me from seeing.

His little face had tipped up, watchful.

Somebody whistled somewhere in the greenish bright and quiet and someone was asking, *Ready? They've already begun.*

I felt nothing but that they moved me, crudely, my sloppy haunch, hardly mine—the drape seemed to hang to mark the place where my body detached at the sockets.

I listened: this was his being born.

This was the sound of a hand wedged in, and then the small bent head popped free, quick as a tooth you are losing. This that I felt backed into my throat was the body shoved into the cage of my ribs, brief, and how surprising: the rest had seemed so distant: a ditch cut into a distant slab, spongy and geologic, marsh, a bowl of softened bone. Then the baby, the bawling sight of him; then the staples driven in.

Nothing lasts, but nothing is finished either. The brain boils and cools, same as many things, heals with the slickness of scars. Nothing's lost; no grief, unspoken, forgotten.

Yet we hold our tongues. Not a word, these years, about it. Hardly a word between us, even then, my sister and me, the very day, those hours, the long before and after in the back seat to Atlanta, after Phoenix, Daddy driving, after Mother, I think it pleased him, the look of it, his girls, his new wife neatly beside him. He wanted to stop and look at things: Chickamauga, Antietam, the cannons in a row.

Of course I think of it—how it must be, might have been, for Sister, closing in on Atlanta. In the morning, plain tea. The righteous out in the early heat, their foetuses wrinkling in jars. Our father moved to her to take her arm to steady her along. She seemed to straighten: he had noticed her being brave. Had she seen the fluted columns, he wanted to know, the Corinthian scrolling above? She looked up, we all did, and listened, he spoke so little, and spoke of Sherman that day as though they were friends, as though we had him to thank for it, my father, that the building still stood, Georgian and grandly columned, spared—handsome, I remember thinking it then, he was as handsome as when we were girls.

We needed so little from him. To be spoken to, to be steadied, that was extra, that was gravy. Because here already was bounty, I thought, her own crisis, here was her chance to be Daddy's, to be brave, to be seen being brave, being ready.

Here was her act of love.

The worse the march the better. The righteous who strained at the roped-off yard, rattled their jars, a child on a hip, how lucky—something more to endure. Half a year's neglect endured, the wiggy pitching months of it, and now, this late, late as it was, the danger, the night's long labor ahead. The toddlers in the leggy grass, writhing, moaning, *Mommy.*

The day a blaze, the early heat. The bodies yawing sweetly in their lettered jars.

They did not hurry. They were solemn, the two of them, processional: a girl on her father's arm. There was something of a lilt and quickening, something graceful—vaguely—supple, fierce, something punitive and bridal in the way she moved to the door.

She had worn her heels, our mother's pearls. She had worn the dress our mother used to dress for parties in.

I held my tongue; this much was easy. I began for a time to feel it too, a queer sort of pride in myself: I had gone to Phoenix and fetched her home and here we all were with him, quietly, soberly walking. To what, walking to what, it seemed all at once not to matter. What mattered was that we were doing as our father asked. He made it easy, provided; he gave us our instructions.

I flew out. The desert bloomed. I was to fetch her home.

I withheld him, the threat of him, the name in my mouth, to try her. But nothing else I could think of in the days I spent in Phoenix, not love—I trotted out every homily I had heard of the family romance, sacrifice, devotion, the kindness of a kindhearted man (*my mouth* : I was moving between lovers, snorting junk in the sumac behind the corner store)—her own unreadiness, it did not move her, and not the ghoulish stories I knew of babies grown in wrong—the ones who lasted, babblers, maimed, stood up, shipped out to Mississippi.

My god, the lavishness of her Mississippi. Any outrage I could think to relate was an insult, a pittance against it. But I did not know so then. Mississippi was years to come—bodies dropping in the viney woods, *hula hula*, somebody new: a curdling, lunatic glee. We held our ground, the field in bloom, the gate swung shut behind us.

A gate swings shut behind you, going in, if you go, coming out.

They came to us over the open field, toothy, threnodic, multiplying as they moved.

"The baby's fine," she said. "It's going to be fine."

I said, "That baby grows in you."

We roomed for days in a motel in Phoenix, a dry wind scratching the door.

I said, "I was in the airport. I was on my way here to you."

It was something I had heard in the Ladies', talk of the boy, women tipping toward the mirror to slide their lipstick on. I said I had seen the boy, coming to her, his hand in his mother's skirt, a blinker of flesh hung over one eye, eyebrow to nose, the skin crusted and thick and frilled—I went on, I could feel my voice rising—his eye yellow in its socket, wild, what I saw of it, who saw nothing, and the flap as brown as potato, gouged, stiff hair hatching from it.

None of this moved her at all. We drew the curtains, hardly spoke, and watched daytime TV. When the day came to leave there, I said what I had been saving to say, to have it on me, to feel that I had convinced her. It was easy. "Daddy's on his way."

Daddy held her arm, to guide her, to keep her on course for the door. Sister reached behind her back and fluttered out her hand

and I—I think it must have surprised me: that she had thought to reach for me, and then that she had not. I took her hand. She drew me up from behind her to walk along up the walk with them, on Sister's arm, Sister on our father's arm, the new wife trailing behind us. I had not heard her. I had not likely listened. I was hearing, I think, the rest of them, the fathers, daughters, churchly men, the sisters hissing scripture, a vast unholy throng.

I saw her face then: I saw our mother's. I saw her face in the face of another mother gone to her knees in the uncut grass with her baby hugged against her chest in the litter of all they had brought there.

They had labeled the months, the stations: Here is your baby at three months, here is your baby at four months, here is your baby at five.

They were reaching in under the rope strung up to keep them off my sister, to keep them away from me. They were snatching at the hem of our mother's dress. I kicked at their arms, their faces.

"Mother—" she said it loudly, and let my hand go.

I thought she had meant it: *Mother.*

I heard Sister all along, I know, walking along: "Mother." But I had not thought of it. This is how I came to think of it—it made it easy, easier for me: we were sending her baby to Mother. There were not enough babies among the dead for all the mothers to mother.

Sister turned from me; she fluttered her hand behind her back, teetering on her heels.

They bent their heads; they were kneeling, rocking on their knees. I thought maybe they meant to drink from the jars, maybe they meant to sing.

I thought, going on—I knew better: I understood it, the news of it, the reason they had come—but then I thought they had come in need to her; they had come to her to be tended to—it was stupid—to be answered—I knew I was being stupid—to be dropped to their knees and saved.

I saw they had saved out a jar for her.

She began to throw them coins.

"One more."

She touched a forehead. She tossed away a ring she liked. She kissed a boy they offered.

"One more baby more," they said.

She tried to lie down. She thought to let them cut it out of her, the easy way. Who can say now, what I had brought her back over the country to do, what Sister thought she was meant to be doing?

I saw her knees give, she was turned from me. She was reaching for the new wife's hand, calling the new wife: "Mother."

And this surprised me. It was nothing, it was the way of things.

I fell behind some. If it had been me. She tried to lie down. I might have let her.

He got her moving. Daddy was gentle. I could see Daddy meant to be gentle. He had her by her hair. He hauled her up some. He had her by the braid his tidy wife had made of the mess of Sister's hair to keep our Sister nice that day, to keep our Sister tidy.

You think it's easy? The way she tries you. The way she—listen. You think it's easy? You think she means to make it easy? *Sister, mother, holy joe.* To be our father? To keep her moving, swung to her feet and gone?

My guess is they gave her Pitocin, a drip, same as what they gave me. They give you your fishnet panties. Then they send you to wander the halls in your socks until the contractions begin.

There are other mothers out there: it's insulting: that it is not only you. But it must have calmed my sister—to have somebody new to talk to, to lap the nurses' station with.

In time, I talked too. Stood in the gaggle in the yellow glare, rubbing the drum of my belly. Not because I thought I had to (talk)—decorum, no, nicety, not then, not yet again. This was our blessed respite. Nothing decorous about it. Only lassitude, rapture, a flaunted animal pleasure. I'll go on, I went on, I have never been quite so sweet on myself, and talky, in time, and shameless—avid, giddy, apart. I might have told anyone anything. I think talking made me hope to prolong it, stop it, hedge some way—I wasn't afraid, much—the table, the curtain drawn, not even the room, the stirrups, the blank chill of the day outside, none of this really shook me—not the pain, quite, the prospect of pain: I thought, *Come on, come on:* what is the pleasure of what does not cost you, hurt you?—no, the room, I think, thrilled me, the wide belts, the tools, the dim medieval look of it.

When he was in me—that was when he was easiest to love.

They let me blather on, the others. We all of us mothers did. We scrutinized, amazed ourselves, the hearts we grew, the milk, the bone, the ax to wield; the father, yes, *come in, do, gently—there*—helpless there, supremely: remote, absurd, refined. Our faces swelled, our eyes withdrew; we spoke our old lost tongues. This of course was later; this was the fabled room. We were lucid at our station, patient in the yellow glare, divulging in our measured tones the blanching gape of cervix, vying some, even then, predatory, preying, somebody's sticky plug spit out, somebody's bloody show.

Had your bloody show, dear?

Yes, yes—then nothing. Instructions. Nurses, nurses, somebody always grinning from the corner of my room.

I lost hours; they might be years. The grasses sang. The riverbanks shrilled and buckled. I know I wandered. I saw a white horse burning. I saw my mother sleeping in the bend of a yellow road.

Pieces missing, syllables. The living thinned to shadow, droned, busy at my knees. At what?

But who could know?

Even now I worry George to recall to me the day's events; I want orderliness, a story, the discrete before and after.

And after, before the room, the wide window over the Merrimack, dark then, the coming dawn, before they brought him to me—these are the questions that flare in me, petty, absurd—I had not seen him but to see him, plump and bawling, thrashing in the sick light and in whose scoured arms? And who is it who went off with him? What surly, immigrant nurse, mistaken for a mother, bathed him, while I in my decorum lay in the cool with the curtains drawn chatting with the postmaster's wife?

What difference? And yet I think of it. Ought to think instead of Sister, yes, be a good big sister. Easter in the morning. Ought to bundle up in the morning, stash my boiled eggs. It being Easter. Since she is my sister.

Sit her down—she claps at me—show her how to hold him, show her what to do.

Her own, she could have held—a guess—in an open hand—small as that, if she wanted, if she was lucky, if the nurses were on their rounds.

Of course I think of it. I hardly think of it—except that she is here. I think of us in the blaze of heat and of the room where we waited, the chairs we took, side by side, the row of scaly bucket seats bolted to the wall. We tipped our heads back. People do—and there were years of people before us, drooping in those chairs. How lucky: a single salient detail: the plaster worn smooth behind us, stained: years of hair, the press of heads, oily, elongated patches. We were resting, had been, those of us who came to help, to fill out papers, if help was how you thought of it, who waited there, dozing, until we were certain the job was done.

It was done—this is as much as I know or want to. Do not know or ask so much as even was she on the potty, the sheeted bed, the floor? Was it dead or living? Did she have a look at it? I would think you would have to look at it—see was it a boy, a girl, have a name to call it by, count its fingers, toes. Or maybe this is me. Or maybe I don't know. But I think I would want something from it—a thumb tip, a twist of cord, we keepers, not to have nothing at all from it, anything small to show.

She turns her palms up. Supple as he is and weak—what harm? And yet she is my sister. And yet she is my sister.

And there is the favored wingback, stout of arm, of wing, of foot.

I pass him to her. "Watch his neck."

"I know, I know, I know."

Hickory, gingko, willow, elm.

Sweetpea, wicker, junior mint. Little man, I call him, honcho, buster, sugar boy. Almost never Reno, sometimes kid Reno, buckareno, buckaroo.

She calls him Binny. *Heeey, Binny. It's your Aunt Kathleen.*

The bird dog she calls Honey Gal and, before long—because much of the time we call her Snoot, for her snoot—my sister calls her Snout. This gets us laughing, George and me, helplessly, until we are falling out of our chairs.

"Nose," she says, and touches his nose. "Ears. Cheeks. Chin. What's this?"

She spreads her hand on the crown of his head and gives it a turn to show me. "Look."

But it is only the scabbing rash he has had, yellowish and common, thriving between where his eyebrows will be. "And this, what's this?" on the slope of his nose, the puggish end, the hard pale knots of acne. "Uunh."

She lets his head tip back and fingers his neck and it is in my mouth to stop her but I am thinking I understand it, suppose

I do—the hope of finding a flaw in him, some lasting crimson blemish. Even a terrible wrongness, I think, it is not such a stretch to think of it: she is hoping to find her mark on him, evidence of kinship, even if, or especially if, it is the kinship of the maimed.

I stoop over her, look to see what she sees: there is vernix still, I have missed it, gray and ripe and gummy, lumping up in the folds of his skin. My sister draws her finger along a crease and the baby squawks and gags. "That's enough."

Too much for me already. I gather him up. Remember to kiss her. I remember the place at the bend in her arm Mother used to rub before Sister slept, to help her sleep, and I touch it. "Love you great big," I remember. Then make my slow way to bed.

My bed is the bed for winter. I sleep where it is warm.

I wake backed away to the foot of the bed, our boy grunting and snuffling against me. Else I cannot find him—he has pushed off from me in his sleep as I sleep: he has crept into the cold with George.

George sleeps out in the summer-room where we used to sleep before the boy, in the wind and sun, in the trees we like, the sickly elm, the willow, the branches bent to shade the barn we keep our boy's things in. He runs the fan for quiet. He makes a tent, as boys do, of his blankets to read by flashlight in.

Three long walls are windows. He wakes in the cold and trees.

Nights I wake to find George here should he come to me from the summer-room, the room the late-summer gold of corn the afternoon our planets crossed, the day I made my harvest. The baby is between us, or I have lain him, briefly, near, in the wicker bin beside the bed. I reach in sleep for him: I reach for the baby. I pet his face, his tender belly. He pulls me to him. I feel his penis stirring softly in its patch of hair.

Boy, my boy.

But what years I have slept. He is weathered. He is bony, bearded, grown.

They took him from me, to keep him safe from me, early on, while I drifted.

I came as I drifted to a dazzling sow, a slot chinked in her back for coins. In my back, were names I'd forgotten, welted loops and straightaways I could make out with my hand: PRIM SUE, PEPPER, GLORY: the animals when I was a girl.

I'm a dwirl, I'm a dwirl: my boy scamps through the house—in a heartbeat, shall, the brief day gone. *Sthla, sthla, mbla,* he learns, and swings to his feet in the crib.

I had them roll me in my bed against the window: *Let me drift.* I went willingly, unafraid of the cold, my hospital gown with the stamped-down name lapping against my back. The river whinged and gurgled. I skirted the ice at its weedy bank, a selvage poorly sewn.

The baby kicked in me. He would throw his foot through the cut in me, flail through the ragged mouth.

And then? And then?

Instructions. My father in velveteen robes. Presiding, intent on a girlish descant: How to love and hold your tongue. Above him—no cloud, not a tree for shade—I watched my life, a plains bird, circling. *Hello down there. Hello.*

My boy appeared on the riverbank. A dull kite snapped in the trees.

The sow would make her way out through the thicket, I knew, a pig-pretty face, glistening, and drag up the stairs on her hooves. It was the way of things, the way they come at you, I heard the coins tinkling in her belly. She would come at me with her snout.

We stole the bedsheets, a towel, the hospital gown, anything marked we could carry. The fishnet panties, they gave us, and Q-tips to dab his umbilical with, and the bottle with its hooked spout.

We waited the month and then some and by and by George came to me from the summer-room in his slippers. He lay the baby in the bin beside the bed. I felt him push at me. He was eating his way back into me. The old story. You want to creep back, creep back, feed at the spangled shore. My stomach fisted. Seized, contracted. I breathed, a pant: the huffing the nurses teach you. The body going on. He kept on, the good George, so patient, so brave, I felt his brain beat in my knees. I felt him tire; I held him to me, the baby crowning, folding apart on his tongue.

She came on, the sow, she blapped through the door, rearing. She was tall as a man and grotesquely smooth. Her breasts were a pinkish girl's.

I lit into her with my umbrella, I beat her about the head. I was blazing, vile, a blinded heat. Still she charged, charged again, rutted at me with her snout.

It took hours of beating to kill her and when I had killed her I hauled her out and threw the bolt on the door.

Still she lived. She clawed at the door and simpered. *A cigarette, dear:* her last request, her voice a child's. I softened. I crept the door open. She was swaddled in cellophane and wearing a bridal gown. Her eyes were sockets, sooty, gone—the soupy mass flushed out. Her breasts were lumped and spitting milk. *Dear, my dear.* She would never die. She would die at my door forever; she would wait me out.

We rock for a time and I lie with my boy and listen to the talk downstairs. The good George. Sister telling of her weekly sweetheart; she has had a belt tooled with his name. And what, George asks, do the two of them like to do?

"Goof around. Eat popcorn. Listen to music," Sister says.

One day, she says, they will marry. They will have a big house and a horse in the barn and their children will learn to ride early. And dogs, oh they will have lots of dogs, and too many cats to count or name, and geese and such, and heaps of corn, and her children—mercy, let them, fine, she isn't going to fuss at them if they want to play tag in the garden.

She has brought me two spores of kudzu to force in the windowlight through the trees. "From home," Sister says, morning then, the coming melt, *hooome*—a drawl, a dipthong, our lie. A little something, a little green in the house when the cold has come—*from the heart of Mississippi*.

Seeping, cloistered bottomland. The spores loosen. Look— they are dropping through the trees.

You would have to burn down the delta to stop it.

And do what, to stop our Sister?

She makes her way in with a sickle, hacking at the matted vine. The spores shake loose—a sack of eggs, a thickish rind, a warty bulb that roots, divides, in the loam where it touches down. They find Sister fallen to sleep in it—in the broad, sweet leaves, the ghosting, the heads of the trees grown over, grown into, disappeared.

Hearsay from Mississippi. We make our few brief visits.

I swear and swear to do better, and Daddy does, and Daddy's wife, and doesn't Sister have her vocation meantime, her piece work they give her to do—bagging dirt, sorting screws, packaging tobacco? Tasks for the able of body and mind, for the residents who stir from their chairs.

The boy I remember best doesn't. "He's gone by—" this is how Sister will say it when I ask— "He went on by last week."

He is spindly, pretty, his mouth licked clean, a boy grafted to a shabby chair. He sings, and drives and drives a Matchbox car across snapshots of his family.

Honk and the gate glides open. A pond, a rolling green. A hatching of beds for flowers, the crepe myrtle in bloom.

And then they come at you, falling out of the trees for you—flapping arms and twisted, torpid, ruinous mouths.

They flopped themselves onto the hood of my car, shrieking, pleased, *hula hula*—somebody new, some mother, hawker, hapless holy joe.

Some stingy sister. I sat at the wheel with my head in a vice while they battered and stroked the windows, my boy not even in me yet, my belly flat and still. And still it seemed to look at them would spread their sickness to me, saddle me with mother-dreams: ears knuckled stubbornly in the column of a boy's limp neck; hands like melted plastic, paws, paws, repeaters, spit swinging from their mouths.

Yes, yes, we will visit. Make our slow way down.

How better to feel lucky? To list my missed afflictions, his: no blighted limb nor burgeoned lobe, no purple stain: to gloat?

And yet I must know better. Things take their time to show.

Baby okay? Baby okay?

Just ducky.

I hear the piggledy snort in the loam. Then sleep—in the shallows, in the grievous sweetness of milk on his breath.

Before long they will mount the stairs, George in his boiled slippers, Sister hauling the dog. "Hey! What do you think you are doing, huh? Quit that. Gooood. Hey."

George is trying, gently, to hush her. It is like trying to hush the wind. "What did I just say to you? You stay. There. Hey. YOU. COME. RIGHT. HERE."

The baby stirs, and paws against me.

Outside: a growth of fog, a glaze of sleet on the windows.

I sleep again, pretend to, when George eases open the door.

I watch him undress in the windows, fast, in the cold of the summer-room—a boy with his flashlight burning, diving for his bed. I go bed to bed, boy to boy, as I wish to, as I must.

Baby sweet, sweet night. Something nibbles, drags its tail through the walls.

They will come to me—days I cannot stop shaking. Burgundy at noon. He is toddling, too young for school, strapped into his seat in the car. *I hate you, Mama. My heart hates you.* I am driving. To keep him safe from me. Keep him safe from harm.

Sister turns in her bed, the dog nested.

The animals asleep in the barn. Used to be.

Used to be I whinnied. I was a girl who whinnied. Slept out in the field with the broodmares, springtime, foaling time, a stick at my side should the coyotes come, longing for the night's heroics.

Sister asleep and walking, used to be, water for the rabbits, a pot to scrub, the garbage dragged to the barrel where we burned. Her shoes buried. A stash of food beneath the bed.

My bonnie. My bonnie lies over.

We had a music box for our necklaces. A ballerina beneath the lid. Little caketop, little throwaway, mesmeric, smooth and pink and poorly made. Little glory. A life's beguilements. She sprang up before the mirror—endlessly, shamelessly spinning.

If you wake Sister, you wake her screaming. Something you ought to know.

Months pass, whole seasons pass, my boy caught, clasped to the bed, a clockhand, he turns, searching for me, his mouth pulsing—in the watery murk of a car swung past, the slow sweep, a dappled shade, the great leviathans circling.

Sister is singing, a few odd hollow wavering notes, out on the glistening shore.

I draw the bedsheets back. It is winter yet, I can hear them: the small, furred bodies in the walls.

The wind has risen. Ice crazes in the trees.

I find Sister down the hall in the bathtub, in a dusky wash of grime and blood, sudsing with the dog. She has got the candles burning. The dog whimpers when I open the door.

"Just checking," I say.

Well and good. Good enough.

"Good night, then," I say.

"I'm just washing her. She likes it," Sister says.

"Yes."

"She likes it. See?"

"Well, goodnight," I say.

"Where is Messpot?"

She calls him *Messpot. Young'n. Binny. See? I am right here.*

I see she has ground out her cigarette on the blotchy rim of our tub.

"He's asleep," I say.

"Like a baby. I gave him a soft goodbye."

The dog lunges, "HEY," tries to. Sister hauls her down by the collar, water slopping onto the floor.

"It's late," I say. "I'm tired."

"So you won't sit with me."

"No."

"I thought maybe."

Might have, yes, maybe—in the humming, the distant ward, might have brushed her hair, mothered her, a girl without a mother, laboring in a tub.

I swing the door shut.

She tried to lie down. Daddy had her by her hair.

He had her things heaped up in the room Sister claimed in his house by the time we reached there. I was to clear her out, drive her south to Mississippi—withered fields, the cotton picked, the river dropped and chalky. *Home.*

I packed Sister's figurines for her, the pale little porcelain boxes she kept, the dingy china dolls, amused, their vacant breakable faces, their broken hands and shoes, their bodies cloth beneath their gowns, flimsy, durable, sewn. Our grandmother's sorry slippers, I packed, and the bundles of letters a boy had sent, some darling, new for a time, the ones I hadn't stolen from her that Sister was waiting to open.

A little something, baby. All I'm asking, the boy wrote.

Token, talisman, caketop, stone. Anything small to rub or suck, to hoard—a nut, a buckeye—I packed. A china doll, a Matchbox car: easily lost, renewably dear, something to grieve, lament at last, the breakables, perishables, bloody plugs and silken locks, the rheumy gristled button plucked, the newly born, the newly dead: first and last and only.

Send me a word or something. José needs a kiss or two.

We kept the windows down—Sister healing, rank in the heat—and her hair, pulled free, was carried upward, out. A great bristly shank of it hovered and plunged above the roof of my car.

A day at the lake, a battlefield. And then the bright gates swung open.

I pull the door shut, move away down the hall.

The baby is waking, whimpering—*quick!* Then the trumpet, the sound like an elephant charging.

I make my way to him. Lie down beside the boy, against him, animal to animal. Anyone would do.

It is not lost on me, not lastingly: anyone would do. *Nurse Jane, Nurse Jane, Nurse Alice.*

I am food, heat, a smell to him; a teat in the dark, a plug in his mouth. No matter the claim, no matter what tenderness moves me. He moves to the smell he left on me, the mark he knows me by. Little monkey. Little brain on a stalk.

How can it be he lives?

He is impossible, embryonic again in the simple dark—doomed, suddenly, mouthy, gilled, unready, misshapen, unmoved.

My one.

Brain in my brain, heart in my heart. A dimpled leg, ten fisted toes.

I did not know mine from another's.

Yet he thrives, plump, deep in the gorgeous, ruinous lie: nothing lives but that he lives too. Nothing stirs. Not a wind, no bird in the stippled wood—but that he cries out, that he sees.

Such a world. The sun sails past, warm to the touch. His body tethered, flown.

Now the moon.

What of the sea, the barn adrift? The fallen, throbbing stars?

Try crying, cry out: a shade appears, a dolorous tide, darkens the window, swallows the sky. A mothering heat, a shadow bent.

Feed and she will vanish; cry and she appears. Not a rib, not a bang. Only whimper. Small god.

I am emptied out.

Shaken loose, how swiftly—George is coming to me down the hall.

He smells of Naugahyde, of ready food, the distant rude perfumey press and beery lure of airports, of bodies on the move. He drops into bed beside me, emits a gassy sibilant conciliatory whisper.

Then he is on me. The baby jostled awake, watching up, hairy papa, pleased.

I pinch my eyes shut, not to laugh at them, at how they must look to each other, how they look to me. George is wrestling my pilly nightgown free, rolls me, hurried, dogged, gone—but that Sister is screaming: "WHAT DO YOU THINK YOU ARE DO-ING, HEY?"

George stops a beat and we listen: she drags the dog back into the tub.

Two beats, three, another. Sister sings. The dog sputters and coughs.

Poor panicked hound, slipped free, hauled back. *A dog devoted, briefly loved, gone to the Post Everlasting.*

Yes. Tell it, Sister. The gods shine down.

She is a Miracle, soon to be, a gospel girl in ribbons and pearls: a Miracle in Training. Cheerful Helper. Much Improved. Miracle in Training.

George rolls off me: he has remembered—where he is, and who.

Husband, father, suitor, son.

Resolute, a man in need. Thinks: give it a go. Hup, boy.

He takes his time for a time, he is easy, he is breaking softly into me.

I would stop it. Send him off down the hall, down the hill, Sister in tow and the dog behind and every last goodly neighbor, everyone else who means well, everything else that needs.

Just the one, I want—shoeless, a girl, her tongue cut out—to slip food under our door. Not a peep. Leave me to molt and heal. I have bones again, I'd forgotten—joints—gristle, sinew, glassy balls drifting in their pockets. The lifted blue of my veins recedes. A man-sized thumb in my belly unmoors—a nudge at the hull, a nosing; a ghoulie, a ghostie, a bump in some fattened tube.

Buck up.

George turns me away, not to see, should I weep. "Stay with me."

Say *mine* again. *Gimmit, do.*

The rest of life before us.

Sit tight. Lie back. Lucky you, you feel it.

I have kept to my chair to feel it—what hook is set, what press desists, what frightened, woozy, ravening love bends its back against us.

"Where are you?" George says. "Stay with me."

Our boy bats at us, god of us—his blessed farce.

I say, "I am right here."

Here to please. A girl, a mark, caught again, my wrists cuffed above my head. George is working up to it, working slowly in.

I give in, gave in. It is my habit, my dodge.

He had me pinned, this George, another, pricked, Andy Petie Billy Bob, the way into me dry and narrow.

"All your little friends," he said.

Pig-eyed boy, he smelled of hay.

"It's a matter of time," he insisted.

What isn't?

Soon—a plea, a girl spliced in: virgin girl on a spongy pier, *how you? what's your name?* hardly matters, fly right, it's a phase, call it that, a passage, christ, what's it for if not?—little vestibule, shrunken, bloody, windswept maw and why fuss after all—it will knit, tell her that. Little whisperings: sing, why not—something plangent, try, to ease her: the cranes flown south, the murmuring flocks; her name, something sweet, hang the sheet out: *his:* that's his flag in my yard, his hand at my mouth, my brash little lollipop of blood, and I am fifteen, the wind in the leaves, the brackish, lurid face of the pond, the birds circling. The dead horse gnawing the barn. Girly, look. *There there there there.* Say *mine* again, our little sweetnee hushed, hooked on a tit, he swipes at me—and *yours* and *yours*, keep your eyes snapped shut, your back to the door, thar she blows, hip hey, girly, look. All your little friends, girl, look, you think you're what?—all your life, because it's nothing, hey, we got babies—red ones yellow brown, four of everything they are making, lord, scissors knife staple string, a nurse in the wings, hup up. The dogs panted, frenzied, dodging him, a boot to the snout, he kept his boots on, shy, he was kind, tell them that, he meant to be kind, conciliatory, pig-eyed boy, and what? this was what? half your life since, bet, half your silly life ago, and he is going, gentle, cautious, gone, husband, father, suitor, son. Christ, the stink of it, the tedium, the final blind obliterating rut, and the dog cries out, the dog breaks free, hysteric. She would drag the boy out by the scruff of his neck, paw a hole for him in the yard, half a chance; and Sister, here she comes, Sister blunders in, weeping, she is naked, "YOU," wet from the tub, hot on the trail, like the time, like the time, our little tribe, what a sight, little sweetnee boy, buckaroo, will you look?—buckareno, pleased: heat; teat and maw. The muscled sack, galactic. A mind blown out, the shimmering hoard. I am cellular, moldered, spall. Moss and stump, silt, a stream. Dewfall, a pebble turned. Viscera and brine. Oocyte, fiber, hindmilk, fore. The body's yield and issue.

He cries: my milk springs forth. George laps it up in a rapture and the dog dives under the bed.

They are restored to their places when I wake again, the room hushed. Nothing to hear but the baby, the jubilant, garrulous moon.

I fetch the basket from the foot of our bed. A little something. I think it is something a sister might do: bring a basket—grass of tinselled plastic, a few wrapped chocolate eggs.

The light is still on in the bathroom, the water still in the tub. A streak of her blood on the toilet seat, Sister's fingerprints on the wall. And in the hallway: something soft underfoot, a lump, then two, another. I think I am finding animals, deer mice come out to forage at night and caught, our bird dog's habit. I pick them up by their tails, hold them up in the bathroom light.

It is surprising—how little you can tell. But I can smell them, a mineral stink, the legendary filth of menses.

The dog has worked at them to leech the blood, to grind the swollen cotton loose. They ride in her stomach, glossed and turned, grown slick before she spits them up the color of tarnished silver.

I creep the door to Sister's room open.

She has her foot out. Our mother used to sleep with her foot out.

I pull the sheet back. The dog's lip twitches; she yips in her sleep. Sister has a hand hooked in her collar.

"Go outside?" I whisper.

I draw the curtain back, the sky in the trees a weak boy-blue, light enough to see by. I see she has a pile of the cotton pads I keep in my bra to sop the milk. The pads are shredded. She has found a bra the dog tore up and a plastic diaper cover too.

She has my gown on. On her pillow is the mangled snapshot I have learned to expect to see: the newly loved, the newly dead, a name in her hand across the back, the boy's name: Joe Young. She will pull it from her pocket and speak to it when George ferries her back to the airport: *I'm coming home, Joe Young.*

Her duffel's open. Two spores. Socks: one pair. The raggedy peel of an orange. She has brought her makeup case, *my kaboodle,* she calls it, locking, big enough for shoes. Cowboy music and a hymnal—so she can practice: make the cut, the bus.

They go by bus, the Miracles, mouths pressed against the windowglass, plying the river towns. They wear their leather bracelets, tooled: W.W.J.D.?

The mark of the exalted. The innocent, the maimed.

Sister wears hers in her sleep, I see—should she wake in the street, the rain coming down. Should you find her. She has wandered off, her house in flames. Her ribboned hair freshly curled.

W.W.J.D.?

Let it be a question.

What would Jesus do?

A little something, baby. All I'm asking.

I try to think of something to take from her, to give to her, the towels I took from the hospital, mementos, what have you, the drift of things, the sock stuffed with rice for the suture, I think, to lay across it, warmed, a balm to me, a smell like buttered toast. Let Sister strew rice through the house, I think, make a trail, tattered foil and tampons, the shells of the eggs I have boiled for her, dribblings, her mark. The body's gluey excess.

Here. You got me here.

I will find her with the sock with the toe eaten out and pretend she has failed to be grateful where gratitude is due.

I slip her Jesus bracelet off.

Make a deal with myself, with Sister, the gods. I will teach her how to hold him, how to bathe him, what to do. How to tend the stump of umbilical, the pasty, toughened button. It is turning on its tether by the time Sister flies in.

You draw the nub back, the button. Take an easy sweep at the healing root with a cotton swab.

Don't be afraid of it, I will tell her. I tell her what Nurse Jane told me. Nothing to snip, to tuck or stitch. Nothing to be alarmed about.

Come light, first thing, when I am tidy yet, rested some, stronger then, scrubbed. The night behind us, breakfast on the stove. Sister will come down swinging her basket, pleased, and take her place at the table.

Somebody new to talk to. Somebody new to listen. Sister, listen.

We left the house first thing in the morning, I will tell her, salt on the roads, the blank of the day, a foot in the cage of my ribs. We crossed the river—once, twice, crossed again, for the feel of it, the sweep through the fog; for the time it took, the scrap of a chance to be ready.

I didn't know what to feel. What would it be to love him, to tend to him, never to be alone again, my own again, never to be without him? Still to wake and find him gone. A curtain tapping at my window.

This was our house when you were a boy. Here is the bed you slept in. When you waked, you shouted, It's morningtime! and we lay in our bed and listened for you—coming to us, bright boy, running to us, for the sound of your feet in the hall.

She will sing to him, coo at him, bounce him on her knee, the baby palsied—her whole body going, his. "Whee hee hee. Whee hee hee."

Oh don't worry, Binny. Don't you worry, Binny. I am right here.

Sister turns in her sleep, moaning. At her throat: our mother's pearls.

"I saw her sleeping."

I say it aloud, whisper it—to hear how it might sound to her, how it sounds to me. "I saw our mother sleeping at the bend in a yellow road."

They wheeled me off from him. They wheeled him to me—
swaddled, scrubbed, still as death in his Lucite bucket.

Nurse Jane wheeled him to me. At her throat, a string of
pearls. First light, white world, the blind at the window sprung.
Little bird.

The day clapped shut. The river turned and gurgled.
I thought I had lost him. I thought if I never saw him.
They drew the curtain across my chest.
No moon. The light popped, the room stuttered out.
Maa maa. Want to jump on rocks?
I called out for a nurse.
Nothing doing.

I slip her pearls off, her glassy ring.
"Little bird," said the nurse, "little keeper."
"Nurse Jane."
She lifted him out to show me, pleased: no X where there
should be a Y, no extra smudge of either. No stump of gray, vesti-
gial tail, no show of sticky bone.
No moon. Not a sun I could see.

You think it's easy?
I kicked at their hands, their faces.
I wanted to go out swinging, wild, and knock off their heads
with my saber, bawling Sister's name. In the name of dumb heroics, of the bold Tecumseh's boys.
I will let her hold him. Tend to him. A deal, a balm, the pretense,
our lie. I make a game of it—of pretending she will not hurt him.
I make my offering: the band at his wrist, the name my
name, a loopy, girlish cursive. Orderliness, a story. Something to
think of us by.

"Nurse Jane tidied my bed, humming," I say. "She seemed to bleed from her ears."

I bend to kiss her. I kiss the bright patch above Sister's eye, a scar from when we were girls.

You will take good care of your sister? Mother asked.

Her children loose in the world.

No harm. All's well. Nurse Jane. Come light.

I would have destroyed him—when he was in me, pod, stalk and sponge, not to have him be like her, not to be as I am with her.

Her mouth is open. I think to spit in it.

I think of us in the quiet, the blessed antiseptic cool. The nurse standing by to wait for her. You have to wait for her.

She draws her foot back. Such a pretty girl, our Sister. So easy, for a moment, to love.

I bend to kiss her, I kiss her gently.

I think of how she called to me; she pressed my hand to her belly.

"See?" she said.

I said nothing. Nothing came to me.

Nothing comes to me now.

The baby kicked and swung in her. He was having a good hard romp in her before they got him out.

I stood and felt him. The nurses whistling, padding about in pneumatic shoes, music on the PA. Sister hummed a bar, how like her.

And then he quieted. I think to hear her. I swear I think he quieted to hear the bit of a song she knew.

I leave the basket. Get out before she wakes, I think, go down to dip the eggs.

And yet she wakes. I press the pillow against her face—to calm her. It has calmed her for years: to have something soft to scream into.

She thrashes and shrieks and I hold her, wait for her to twitch off to sleep as she does—on the instant, the disconnect, the body jerking free.

Then I go down to dip the eggs.

I dip them briefly, pallid blues and yellows, enough to be seen in the snow. It is early yet, the plows have not come. The wind has not come from the sea yet and the snow is crusted over.

I pull my boots on, step out.

The yard is shining. Everything is shining, throwing off light from the snow. The trees are bristling. The crocus are showing through. The first of the jonquils bloom and droop and the thrush in the trees come back to us out of the hot, flat land.

I put two eggs in the birdbath. Another behind the gutter-spout behind its gout of ice. I put a blue egg in the bottommost limb of our front-yard beech. The limbs are bent and glisten. The tips of the limb are cased in ice that rises from the crust of snow.

I bowl an egg gently across the crust so as not to leave my bootsteps leading to it to give it away. Just the one I bowl. To make it difficult. The rest are easy.

I take my time some, the baby asleep, the plows groaning out on the highway. It seems to me a blessing to be out in the bright and cold. I bask in a patch of sunlight; wave at the good reverend passing, peddling off on his bicycle bearing the bright calm lamp of his head.

I hide the last egg, open the door. He is screaming.

I find her lying in bed with the baby, my bed, a cigarette smoking on my bedstand, my gown in a heap on the floor.

"I was trying to—"

She can't talk right. She's got the nub, the gristled button, tucked away in her mouth.

I sweep a finger through. She was trying to what?

I don't ask her. She didn't do anything, she was lying there, she found it dropped to the foot of his sleeper. No use in trying to ask her: did she yank the nub loose or gnaw through the leash, take a bite of his hide, so sweet, so soft you scarcely know you have touched it?

I feed her—coffee, toast, get her out and away, searching for eggs in the snow. The dog by and by learns to carry the eggs, to hold them gently in the heat of her mouth with her narrow tongue. She bumps one along to Sister, bowls it with her nose.

The snow moves in a slab to the lip of the roof. The barn is steaming. The grasses appear—in the sun, risen up, a friend to the earth, in the wind blowing in from the sea.

I keep Sister out there. I make her find the eggs, bored or not, after I have gone to the trouble of hiding them, before we go back inside. I found a cap for her, a coat and gloves. I'd have found Cinderella's glass slipper for her to keep her out of the house for a time.

George passes through the window with the baby. They are happy, drifty perhaps. A man and his boy. I hate to see it.

The blooms perk up. The day slackens.

Our old beech groans and tosses its head. We hear the bristle and click of ice on its boughs—a squirrel has lunged and, sluggish, missed, and the body is dropping through.

We move in. Afternoon. The dog dreaming. The baby asleep on my chest.

Sister takes a nap in the sunroom, ribbons in her hair, gorged on sweets, her cache beneath the bedsheets, the chocolate rabbit nested yet among the bright sweet beans.

I walk Sister into the pines when she wakes, the orderly rows, her fingers hung in my pockets.

No sun much, dusk coming on. No wind where we are to speak of. A thrush somewhere, silvery, sings. The boughs are still laden with snow.

And then a squirrel chirps, a clump of snow breaks free. The dog springs like a deer through the timber, squealing, demented, a grape-sized brain, Sister lurching after, the squirrel going limb to limb. Quick as that.

A great wet clump is falling. She keeps her face tipped up to watch it, watches it to the end.

The dog rears up and swoons as she does and hooks a paw over each shoulder, kisses Sister on her neck, on her ears. She picks Sister's—George's—cap off, lopes away snapping the cap in her teeth as though it is something to kill.

By then I've reached her. Sister splutters, spitting out the plug of snow. Her mouth is bleeding. Her face is the grotesque of a face, a soul in flames, some rung of hell, and she is sobbing, spit puddling under her tongue.

I sink to my knees beside her. The Keeper, the Tender: the cheap tableau. "Let me see it."

On her forehead, the abraded skin is grainy with blood. "Poor girl."

I bend to touch her. But she is up, what fun, lunging away, stupid thing, elated. She pounces at me, forgetful, or not—it's that I am feeble still, tender still, careful. I have been told to be careful.

Sister pants: a dog: I never see it quite: who she is, means to be, monkey horsie walrus bear. She rears up and kisses me.

I take a swing at her.

It is the hour, the light, it must be—the sly animal weight of it, amnesiac, the seizing, the night sky clamping down. Fevers rise, hunting time, predators on the move.

I try to get the dog to come to me, come sit by me. I think maybe this will calm Sister, if the dog comes and sits very quietly, she is trained to, you can't know.

I know I have not had my pills yet. I have taken the last of the pills I had that have been, while I heal, a help to me, in the eveningtime in particular, dark coming on, the flattened trees—to dull the ache, the progress, the healing meant by the mess I pass, the sheeny clumpy liverish ruin that is left of being sufficient, of having been, for a time, sufficient, for a time, I swear it, calm.

A body needs something.

Sister wheezes, pets at me. I stop and wait for it: her odd little sudden chirping cry, her drawn-on cartoon mouth.

And then I hit her. She is the way she is and has always been and how she will always be.

And so I hit her. I had forgotten. You forget how it feels to hit somebody like you used to when you were young.

No moon, dim world, the sky velour. A bird above us, circling. We make our way from the trees.

The reverend streams past, slush flung up. Gone to vespers, gone to God. Perhaps he hears her. Thinks not. It is the hour, the light. The wind in the trees. And yet it comes to him; he must remember it—crossing back, going home—to supper, sleep, to his wife, a dream—he must have seen it: the snow in patches, the stain on the snow: the trail she leaves walking back to the house, Sister bleeding into her hands.

"Now, now. There, there."

We cross the street, the welts of slush. The light in the kitchen is burning. The windows are steamed from the heat of something George has set to cook on the stove. Still we can make him out with the baby. He is sitting in the kitchen with the baby, looking out across the road.

It comes upon me—the old, gone way we used to live, how we lived outside until dark came on, until Mother called, the dogs at our heels, the horses fed, the hay in the rustling barn.

We pass the bed of slackened blooms to pass unseen through the windowlight to watch George sitting inside. I see Mother at the sink then also, Mother at her labors, at the washing, at the meals—young still, pretty still, laughing. I remember myself in the spindly dark, the lee of the hedge, the sweetened smell of the harrowed rows turned in the fall in the ripened fields. I spun myself out in the clovery dark; I felt myself thin and wobble. I lay on our land like a fog—upon every fence and creek and stone, every leaf and fallow.

I watch our George in the blaze.

"You know I saw you," he said. "I never meant to. They had you opened. He was spun in his sack and looking at me, blinking, lodged in the saddle of bone."

The dog whimpers. Sister kicks a pale stone at the barn. A dry hush in the limbs and a nicker.

A pine is down in the street. We see in the gray, in the grainy dark, the seepy luminous tear in the trunk that the head of the tree as it fell has torn—all trunk now, that tree, a hollowing snag, a yellow gash that, as the woods grow dark, tips and floats and burns.

I swing the porch door open.

"Aren't you cold?"

"No."

"Not hungry?"

"Uunh."

Sister moves off, calling the dog out slowly.

time for the flat-headed man

It has come to me to introduce tonight's reader.

My wife asked would I. She said it's easy, easier for you, you do it easily. She makes it difficult—to stand here, to open her mouth, it's a struggle, she says. I said, Yes, dear.

Yes hello, dear. Our director. There she is, everybody. Give a wave.

You mostly know me. What I mean to say. I know some of you from class, I see, the ones I've been thrown, I see you out there.

I'm not ungrateful. It can't be easy. For my wife, I mean, not to seem, you know, it's very delicate—she is partial, she's not impartial, after all, no sense pretending. Still she has managed to throw me work. It clears my head some—to stand up here and talk to you in a grownup sort of way.

We have, as you know, the two children. The girl, a boy. They are thinking she is going to get better, our girl. Give her time, they say, some months to grow—

Yes, come in, come in. I'm glad you made it, every one of you. Blinking into the snow.

I was talking about our children. The girl, a boy.

I taught our boy to ride his bike. That was nice. He skids out, lays a patch, wants to show me. Shows everybody his scabs. *Lookit look*: a scab on every joint he can get to. Point of pride.

He says, "Our baby's name is Noodle and I like to suck her hair."

And so he does, I let him, no harm in that. He sets his lips around the hole in her headbone, slurps in a satiny frill. I think she likes it.

How nice to see you. You few I know. You look lovely, really you do. Hello, darling up there. I like your muffler. I like your hats and shoes.

She missed the winters, my wife, it's why we came here. She missed all the different clothes—the heavy coats, the bundling up. You could pass your long life in a halter top in the town we came north to get out of.

The air velvet. Squinch owls and duckweed, pickled eggs. A pontoon boat with the radio on making laps on the side-by lake. Our boy was small there, he was a baby. You could sit him in his bucket on the lakeside in the sun. We had egrets. Once a wood stork. Peahens on the roof of the cabin—tatting at the nailheads, the pipe coming up. Anything bright they could get to.

She comes from Akron, tonight's reader. Akron by way of Toledo. By way of Mayor's Income. That's in Tennessee.

She writes poems. This is my introduction. Wrote a book of

stories, skinny thing, lot of white on the page. She's got two kids same as our two kids. A good gig in Tuscaloosa. A hottie in the chute, have a look at her, some lanky buckaroo. It's what I've heard.

You ever hear of the ones they break the bones on young to get them back set right?

And it works!

While they're small. Little miracles. Such a miraculous day and age with all they know and do.

Hey and look. They are spot fucking on with this weather—it's doing just what it is supposed to do. Your wintry mix. The old standby. Three feet on the ground and now it's—raining swords, our boy says. You've got to really run.

I said Akron, right? She writes poems. Said that. I don't get out much. I've half forgotten—what it feels like, what all I mean to say.

Our boy said, "Papa."

We were lying in bed and he was messing with himself, his little package, trying to make the hole bigger he said. "Papa, look." He stretched it up to show me. "Doesn't it look good?"

His *woowoo*, he used to call it.

"In a few days your woowoo will bloom into a thousand flowers."

He's got the skin on still and he forces it back and out comes this purple ball. It looks all wrong, it looks rotted.

He says, "When you die I hope you're a frog and I will catch you and I will keep you in my bucket."

I liked to think of him there in the heat where we lived rounding up snakes and frogs, growing up, fishing. Little bare-backed nutbrown boy. Swinging through the trees on a strangler fig. I liked thinking of him being a man there sitting on an over-turned bucket.

He'd have a pontoon boat. He could think there. He'd have a radio, a little old crackly transistor of the sort that will hang in your shirtfront pocket. A gentle man. A party of one, making his pointy rounds.

A simpler life.

Of course we're lucky. It is easy to feel pretty lucky. I think she likes it, my wife, this job of hers, directing. It isn't easy, I think you see that, all the details, all the many tiny important things a woman of our day and age has to do.

Plus a mother, don't forget.

Plus the baby. She's not old enough, the baby, you can't break them yet, little buttery bones, no sense pretending. So we keep her stuffed into her harness. Keep our chins up. As per. We think in pictures. It's a help.

She wags her arms a bit, but otherwise—

I'll just say it. I'm not cut out for it, we're not. I mean men, I mean. We're cut to gather. Gather and hunt and think—I used to think, have a thought through in my chair. My chair! Shoved into the corner of my room.

I lay the girl down at the back of the house, pull the door to, steal away. Have a sit.

She has to lie there. She's just little, little bunch, just a nugget. I could drop her through the mouth of the woodstove, be done with her in a day.

Who am I?

Because who am I really, do you think, to her?

She's just little. She doesn't know me. Give her time, time enough, some months to grow, she will point me out, say, "Bapa." The ennobling moment.

The blow to the head. Then the knees go.

Like the heartbeat, first time, the first picture, her little face full on through the tissue, the fiber and brine, and she waved. *Here I come,* she seemed to say, *don't try to stop me.*

You do what you have to do. Burn through. Drop into my hands, big Papa's hands, and he flinches. I gave her up to her mother: glistening, blue, the cord in my hand still humming. And her mother's first word? *Luscious.* Think of that.

They say it's easy, it is all she knows: harness, plaster, spreading bar. Bapa. Hot. Brother. Dog. All the little cups and pulleys.

Her brother drew on her face with a crayon, drew a face.

I was elsewhere. I was taking my ten deep breaths. As per.

You take a breath, keep moving. They can't move, you think you're safe, you think they lie there, okay, and what could come? Well here we come. Bapa. Mama. Brother. Dog.

My wife busts through the door going, "Mama. Come to mama, baby, I'm home."

The old egg clutch. The gladdened hand. She is spitting milk, she is weeping. Bringing the bacon home.

What I like?

I liked lying on the bed on the phone with her, nothing left to say.

I like a good outside shower, looking up through the moss and leaves. Our man in his boat, turning circles. Little lake.

Our lake was shrinking. It was dirtier every year we lived there, the water siphoned off. Lake Rosa. After Rosa.

It was storied. All the good stuff—rape and pillage, dirty Feds. Stills in the woods and sink holes you could drop your murdered through. Gothic excess. I always liked it. I liked the old gin joint sloughing on the banks, the desolated piers. Our boy was small there. Sit him on the slope in his bucket in the sun and the peahens would stroll down and gawk at him.

Then the rumors flared up. Something had killed a peahen, a fellow was missing his dogs. Two, and then another, and then somebody else, and pretty soon they had gotten a posse up and were combing the lake for gators. They came upon an ancient bull in the muck, bellowing and sluggish, and everybody had a go at him, and beat him on the head with pipes. They opened him up and, lookyloo, found a dew claw, hair balls, gizzards. A broken chain of vertabrae, a clutch of radio collars.

A boy bloodied to his elbows, weeping.

The pontoon boat run aground.

I'd say I liked that. The freakish tableau.

The penny in your pocket mildewed.

"Penny?" says my wife.

Nothing to report. A polar cold. The wind chirrups.

Cheer up. Cheer up.

Sugar girl? Forgot your hat! Now get. Safe home. Look both ways twice. Don't let the door hitcha in—

Somebody else? in a hurry?

Scooting out?

Nice to stand here. Talk to big folks.

Poems and stories, she does both, she does the colonies, the clusterfucks, lunch at the door, a little basket. Qi Gong, Feng Shui, reps at the gym. Have a look at her. Stringy thing, she used to dance, flattened abs, the haunch on her, quite the hottie. But you can smell it on her: she's a mother. She's submerged.

Sniff her out, use your nose: she will have turned some. She will have soured, that's a hint. Something's ferny. They're grown over, grown in. A flicker: then gone. You can't reach them. You can't console them. You touch them and they sink away.

What's to do?

I sweep the floors clean. I make the meals.

Our boy sprints at her. The baby wakes and cries.

The ravaged female. Our Lady of the Mount. Miss DMV.

Fresh from the stirrups. As if.

She's spun up, my wife—a little ball, a webby mass. Maybe she moves some, you try to move her. "Hey?"

But, no, it's nothing, she insists. It's just she's tired.

I'll give you tired, what the fuck. I'll give you nothing.

Sit down, sit down. You think I'm finished?

"I amn't finished," says our boy.

We'll make a night of it—the wide belts, the tools. The wonder, the stunt.

Our poet has got her papers out, the dog-eared book. She'll get up here, find her page. Proclaim the miracle. Another living body in her living body yada yada yada yada nothing but give give give.

YOU SIT.

Let a man have a little fun, why not? Air his mind some. I amn't finished.

"I amn't going to hit you," our boy says. "I amn't going to kiss you. I amn't going to get a sword and chop you in two."

"Into what?" I ask.

"A zillion pieces."

My mother's dead now. Which makes life simpler. It is not a joke, it's true.

When my old man was away—he was away quite a bit—I used to go to my mother in her bed. I never asked could I. We never spoke of it. She wore a nightgown the planets were pictured on and I knew in the morning, when my father was away, that she would lie in bed and let me pick at the sleeve, at the small gray beads of cloth I came to keep with the hair from her pillow I found and the skiff of foam kneaded to dust that I tapped from the toes of her slippers. I lay in the dark in the bedheat, in the wet bready smell of her, not moving, pretending to sleep. I was a boy, and then not, too old for it, mommy's boy, and disgusted. In my disgust it grew easier for me to picture my mother in stirrups—strapped in, laboring, gassed, while the waxy, molten globe of my head burned through her.

I never touched her: if I touched her she would burst into flames. I lay away from her and felt the seed move in me, heating up, pearly, the flashing tails, the race to the sea. The bliss of sleep mired.

I slept mired, in the puddle I had made, happy and ashamed.

My brother served us waffles each morning and we lay propped up with the TV on and ate them with our hands. I wouldn't speak to her. I wanted to throttle her. I could not stand it: to have a mother: to have grown my arms and legs in her, my cock and balls, gill and lung, every pore and socket.

I wanted to come from nothing, from air, a cloud, the heavens jewelled. The tinted distance.

She sweeps in, my wife. *Hello, hello.* She's a special event, she's a goer.

I report on the daily doings, tell her what she has missed. The shitty baths. The scabs, some stunt. Some funny little peep her baby makes.

I say, "She spent the day on her backside, lying there hoping to grow."

My wife hovers, coodle coo. Then to bed. She's spent. Asleep by the time I get there—dreaming, I guess, of you. Some one of you tamping burning coals deep into her nostrils. You've pulled her teeth out.

And her a mother!

Full grown. Pushing forty, my wife.

"Those are longing," says my boy, and he swats at her breasts. It's not a joke, it's true.

What I'd like?

I'd like a day on that fellow's pontoon boat, a radio, the white-hot marvelous sun. I would lash the helm, keep her circling.

Sun on my ass, blister my nose. Sit and drink some. Think a few gothic thoughts through.

We got fathers out there? You a father?

See? He's going, *yeah. Baby, yeah. Fucking sit there.*

"I mean it," says my boy, "I'm honest. I'm just standing here, I'm honest."

He's at the bedside, the baby howling. His crayons poking out of his pockets.

Sweet doll. Sugar girl.

He'll make it up to her, he'll saw at his trousers with a Lego. He said, "I'm gonna make these littler so when Noodle ever has a baby then her baby can grow into them. Wouldn't that be cool?"

He puts a dress on, very flowery, a lacy thing she is to grow into, should she grow. "And what shall we call you?" I ask him.

He's sitting on the pot, thinking. "I'd like to be Glorious Angel."

And so he is, spinning through the kitchen with his dress lofting up.

And I am Claybrain, Hiccalump, Clumpfoot, Tuk.

A man in need. Could stand a drink. Stand to sit down.

"We lived in Florida?" he asks. "I was a baby?"

"Yes."

We lived in the land of the halter top. We snived in the snand of the lalter snop. Hip. Pop. Pifflewop.

How nice to see you. You're very tall.

I brought pictures. The boy, a girl. You see they're lovely. They are. We keep her dress pulled down. You can imagine—the little stirrups, fresh out, a new girl from the womb. Her feet folded against her shinbone. Stuffed in. She's fileted, looks like, laid open, very clean. Little clean plump butterflied lamb.

Still look. The look on her! Such a beauty.

You drut. Get out, get out, don't think you're sneaking. You and your sneaky friends. You, man. Up. Make tracks.

"Let's get a knife for ourselves," my boy says, "and run out there and stick them."

HA. The rest of you can stay.

Tell you what, here's a tip, we go to market.

Take the baby when you go to market, boys, take her anywhere there are girls. It's a charm. Look at that. Little buddings. You let them pet her. I take the baby down to the pool. You get a daddy in the pool they're a swarm, watch me, little humpy strokes, the water frothing, they walk on their hands, be a horsie, swim me where I can't swim.

I do, and they are kicking, they are breathing fast in my ear.

"And we lived beside a lake?" my boy wants to know.

"We lived beside a lake."

He's forgotten. He's down to stories. Suspicions, omissions. A foreign view.

"And my mother took me out in my bucket?"

"And your mother took you out in your bucket."

"And my mother loved me very much?"

"And your mother loved you very much. And you were her prince. Her angel. And she loved you. And you were all she saw or could think of. And she loved you. You said *ngogn ngogn*. And I loved you. Your papa loved you."

"And my mother set me down in my bucket."

Firstborn, boychild, hoyden.

Mama, Papa, Clumpfoot, Tuk. We make mistakes, give us that. We're only human.

Pin her down, cinch her up. Man the fires. Sweep the floors.

They say a year, tops. That's consolation. They say, "It is all she has ever known."

I say she used to breathe underwater. She was gilled, webbed, rock, a frog. Amphibious. She was larval. Boiled in the heart of a dying star. She knows plenty.

So they forget: what is that?

The child knows plenty.

He is lava, lightning, Black Bart, bear. He's a worm, torn up, a withered heart. T. rex and the woods are burning.

That's him in the tub, hollering—*hollowing*, he calls it, a pirate song: *hardee-eye-yay, hoodee-eye-yoo*. He's got his face bunched up around his eyepatch. He's using his mother's diaphragm for an eyepatch.

"For a boat," he says, "to kill Noodle with. Kill Noodle."

He has got us racing, on the move: marks get set. "You just keep getting faster and faster," I tell him.

He looks up at me—a long look, sweetly, and says, "And you are getting slower and slower, right?"

He wears his tassled hat—which makes the wind blow—which sparks a lightning—which fells a tree.

His mother took him out into the trees one day. This was lakeside—heat and strangler fig, every manner of insect living. Great mounds. She can't get past it. Carried him out in his bucket—a boy in the cool of her shadow, a babe in his mother's arms. Let it go, I say. Well it's hard, it's hard. Hand of God, you could say, but she won't say it.

It has come to me to say it.

Our boy says, "You have to say *I forgive you*."

Forgive me. Shameful of me.

You see she's leaving.

I used to like it—the feeling that my wife was always leaving, that any moment she would pick up and go. I would hear her drive off, I wouldn't stop her. After a time I would find some picture of her and sit with it in my chair. All true, every word—I would speak to her, as though to her, a grown man, a fool. I could make myself feel very sexy, and wanting. I wanted her, the way she tucked her toes against my ankles when we loved, such a simple act, as small as that—I could summon every foolishness, every hoarded sweetness—the near-blue skin of her ankle, nicked—the seaside, I pictured, the tidewashed shore—dewy and silken and pale, the skin, where the elastic of her sock pulled tight, ribbed, an imprint, the tide recedes, you wake alone in the glare of love. I was undone by it, wished to be, easily, in passing. I rubbed out the print, smoothed it away—would, would, never had: a missed statistic: the incidence of men in their kitchens goading themselves to tears. Sobbing in their rockers. *Come on back, baby. Come home.*

It's me!

Your angel, your prince. Dear old breadstick.

They ought to fix that door. We'll all have dreams of it. Hooked shut. Then the stutter and wheeze.

A woman embarked. Stealing away through the wintry mix, we can't stop her. Just as well. We will stay and speak of her.

She wanted sunshine. The very best for her boy, fresh air for her boy. A little sunshine. Ions, photons, vitamin D. Wanted heat. To be limbered and quiet and slowed. Be his mother. His cooling shade, soft, becalmed. The slow marvels, she would give him, the glistening ant, the lizard's coppery pouch; mirage—puddled silver in our road, the box turtles gliding above. Her wild boy singing in a secret tongue, tongue of wind, tongue of dog.

He would have collections: feathers, coins, the crisp skin of snakes. The beak of a bird, a tree frog. A June bug on a thread. The dream of a life she remembered. The owl in the mimosa, the armadillo asleep in the shadows—you could smell them beneath the house.

She set him down. For an instant. Buzzing heat, lakelight, the drowse. The wag of the brittled palmetto. She moved off, a thinking woman. Thought: sinkhole, felon, dengue, flood. Not likely. But what of the limb, the pebble thrown, the interstellar iceball? She thought of the arc: velocity: mass: the mathematics of the cataclysmic. Perhaps the woodstork. The kid with a stick, the hand of God. The orangutang sprung from the zoo. All that. Still she moves off.

He isn't far, she thinks, she could hear him. She can almost even see him. Should he need her. It's just an instant, just a couple, three minutes she needs just to think, she isn't far, really, just to think some, he's in his bucket, rocks a bit but the ground is soft, he may be sleeping, yes, likely, lucky for her, she can think now, counts the minutes—three, four, loses track—and so she milks it, another minute gone, the list in her head, she will turn back, should, he must be sleeping, poor child, the breeze from the lake, coolish to-day, the day pleasing, what is left of it, was, you mustn't blame her. She hears an owl in the trees and turns away, back—spooked—I never liked it, you hear people say they like it—the hoot, the trill, old owlers, out in the cold, a boy at your heels, and here it comes, the great swoop, quiet as a cloud passing.

She went back then. Her boy was shrieking. Strapped in. Just a baby. She had set him down on a mound of fire ants. Like to carry him off, sure you've seen them. Like on the specials? Just the tiniest things but they swarm.

She came sobbing home back through the trees to me, his bucket swinging against her legs.

We got him hosed off. You couldn't touch him. He stuck every place you touched him.

Those little blisters everywhere broke open and they ran. Fire ants, the heat of the day, you see the logic. We got him strapped in and sedated. Bound for the icy north.

Move along. That'll fix it. Build a rock wall, saw the trees down. Mop and mow. Now you've got her, you've got her, she's gone.

The nights were quiet. Cold already and quiet. Sundown, sunup. Not a bird, not a frog.

He crawled, he ran. He had a birthday. Said, "Papa, I am four almost. And after this I will be six and after that I will be ten and when I become fifteen I'll drive and I will drive so fast and then I will be twenty. Then I will have one leg. Old people only have one leg and then I will be dead, Papa, and you will come and save me. I will be in a pond."

We get out of the car, snow coming down, we're rushing. He says, "Wait, Papa. I want to feel the cold."

It's like a knife at your throat, to love them. It is like gathering leaves in the wind.

We want the best for them both, we're like anyone.

The smell of home, the dog at the foot of the stairs. Your wife asleep, your children. Fire humming in the stove.

Or something else. And else again. We think in pictures. The dream of a life we remember and slept through while we lived.

The velvety air. The way the trees crooked down—how easy he would find it to climb them. All boy. A way to think of him. I think of the lake through the trees where we lived, where she lived as a girl, old Angel Oak, the swinging vines, shrimp you could buy on the roadside. Boiled peanuts. Old coot in the steam on the median, his boy fishing the grate at his knees—a string, a hook, a giving stick—happy with that, horsing, we were happy enough to see them.

We could take a week, go see them. Get some sun on our bumpy bottoms, yellow in our hair. Light out.

It's been a winter, don't you say? I would say it. We came out of our house to come down here, our car was gone to the roof in snow. Still we managed, we two.

It's a distance. Quite a drive.

She pulls her eyelashes out. We keep our hats on. She pulls her hair out strand by strand. That's life, I guess, funny workings, not to fret. It's just I'm—

SIT DOWN.

We all have them—little tics and such, how our minds work. Mine.

I'm not an ogre.

Turn's up, I got you.

Give a hand.

You are very kind, you few, our small tribe, it's just us. The last listeners.

A warm welcome. Come on, Amherst.

I give you Akron.

Give up the post.

I'm gone home, going home.

He likes to lie on my back.

You know the specials? We'll watch the specials: the horned; the frilled; the mighty bird-hipped. Ornithomimus, Avimimus. The theropods, the thecodonts. The king tyrant, T. rex.

Boy, his heart really goes.

Allosaurus, Staurikosaurus.

Little god, boy heart.

Liopleurodon—what eats sharks.

You ought to hear him.

Yangchuanosaurus, Megalosaurus, Tarbosaurus bataar.

Velociraptor: the swift.

Troodon: the wounding one.

All the old dead meat eaters.

back, they were newlyweds, the months they spent in New Orleans.

It had been her idea, New Orleans. She found the place, the peevish bird—it slept on a perch on their headboard; her idea, the verandah, them sitting out for julep time in the last of the sun, in the rain if it rained. She insisted. Julep time, dark or light, rain or heat, no matter.

There were people, passersby, music coming up the street, no matter the time, the weather. They were walled-in, swallowed. Hiving, living among. The building scratched and settled, knocked; something ticked or sputtered, broke; something living nibbled. Sarah had not seemed to mind it. She had almost seemed to like it, his first wife—the slubbing in the crusted pipes, the soups tossed over the windowsills. A wheeze, a moan, a zipper zipped. Snakes in the reek and mire—this, this was just the inside, this was in the airshaft. Peel, marrow, gristle, bone; cast-off prophylactic, leaf and clacking oyster shell. Strays came, no wonder, feral cats—her word, *feral*—howling in the airshaft, the bird in a panic, flapping.

Quiet?—christ, forget it.

Better to live on a cul-de-sac. Better to live on a golf course. He liked the sound of the fans on the golf course, oscillant, obtruding—a whir—there to cool the bentgrass greens.

They settled in near the golf course, at the yacht club, he and Sarah, deep into the marriage. He had his work still, the approaching calm. The lassitude of the arrived, he thinks. A guard at the gate. The surrendering hills. And on a day like today, not a bootprint, not a windowshade tweaked open.

Not a yacht for years, for miles, in sight.

The lake is too small, too shallow, made. What there is of yachts is the word itself and an anchor plunged into the grass before the guard house; there are the miles of anchor chain dragged from yawing, sea-tossed ships—authentic—to grace the lighted fountain, the paved ways over the golf course. On every link is an even, talcumy burnish of rust.

Walter's house is the last house, shored up against the hills. Beyond the hedge is the fairway and the slim tower he can see from their bed on the grassy rise. This is the newest improvement out here: a chiming clock, a sweeping light—grand and exact and costly, the replica of a lighthouse.

Had Sarah lived to see it?

He cannot think quite. It would have waked her—the clock going off, the arm of light.

He tries the TV: talk show, talk show, weather.

He calls up the stairs to Helen. Does she think the paper will come today? Has she seen, by chance, his ruler?

He finds his ruler where he keeps it, measures the snow on the bird house, walks to the end of the driveway to see about the neighborhood kids. They quit moving when they see him; they ball up their hands in their pockets.

"Good idea," he offers.

The bigger boy, when Walter speaks, sort of nods.

The boys are building a snowman, scraping snow from the cul-de-sac, picking out bits of gravel. There are patches of grass on the lawn showing through where they have scooped up the snow and hauled it off. The snowman is gray and lumpy, the blonde grass of Walter's lawn poking through.

Walter bends down, holds up his ruler to the bottom tier. "Well," he says at last, "it's coming."

"Yep."

Walter knocks his heels together. He pats both boys on the head, the stiff crop of their flat-tops. "Carry on, men."

Did they not have a chore of some sort, a father to help, a mother?

He finds his ladder, sets it against the side of his house where Helen cannot see him, and wobbles up. He pulls a dead bird from the gutter, rotting leaves, several golf balls. The golf balls, he drops in his pockets. He lobs the bird into the trees.

Another rung, and he can see the fairway and the gray bank of the lake, far off. The old mother up the street comes out, her coat blowing open, and calls into the snow to her children.

He starts down then. The sky has gone chalky. The snow that must be falling seems to be floating up. He hears a door shut.

He found her letters. They spoke gently of him, mostly gently, of how he had turned away. He thought at first they were written for him. He sees her hand, neat, the yellow pad.

His chest feels wound, bandaged. If he looks too long at the ground through the rungs, the ladder bucks and sways.

What a blessing, Sarah wrote, a gift from the gods—to have found such love so late in life. He tries to feel that. *Love's not time's fool.* She had had the words chinked into her gravestone.

He sends a foot down, noses about for the rung. His foot is as stiff as wood in his boot; in his eye is a blurring, lifting flake, a flying, he thinks, insect. But it isn't, he knows that it cannot be: the spot stays, moves, watery, a wingy translucence. It begins, as soon as he looks away, to sweep across his eye.

He keeps his eye shut; he is not frightened. His trees, his house, his car in the drive—he has kept his world in order. His yard is flawless, as smooth as a lake the ladder rises serenely from.

Walter rests a time, moves again. His leg grabs when he moves—an old hurt—heel to puffy ankle, up, a toothy length of chain dragged up through the vein in his leg. He is bleeding into his boot—that's what it feels like. His eye is a stone in its socket.

The good leg—the one he is standing on—gives. Walter crumples, tumbles, the ladder shrilling across the gutter, fast; it doesn't fall quite. He has the sense to let loose of it, to tuck, pitch, roll, an old athlete.

Hey, hey.

Something dullish at first, and then nothing. Walter lies in the snow looking up.

That was nicely done, he thinks.

Not a scratch, not a tweak he isn't used to.

A car slides to a stop in the cul-de-sac, knocks the head off the snowman.

Ah ha, he thinks—the News at last. A peep, a word, in the stretch of a day—is it really so much to ask?

He feels his heart thump in the vein of his neck. He wants to lie there, sleep, the snow twisting down. He waits for the sound of the paper. Waits for the light from the lighthouse to pass.

He had a route as a boy, a bag and a bike. Rode through swelter, flood, freakish snow—people used to. Mere mortals.

But here it is dusking. A cakewalk, inches. But here it is in the leavings, the very tail of the day, before the goddamn thing, flung out, sails out in its seasonal blue and whomps down onto the drive.

Grace doesn't see her father, doesn't notice, hardly saw the snowman before she swung the car into the drive. She can only do so much at once, after all, and Carl, this Carl, he is always talking. If he would hush—he won't, but if he would—she could concentrate and drive.

She pulls the car up to the chainlink fence, steps out; the dogs are barking. She tries to remember their names. She remembers a dog named Brenja she used to fall asleep with in the hay barn, back when they had a hay barn, years ago, horses. Trees up and down the drive.

Grace walks back to the back of the car and lifts the wheelchair out of the trunk. She stands it down in the snow in the drive and, holding her foot against the wheel, pushes apart the wheels of the chair, the arms where Carl will rest his arms. She pushes until she hears the stays lock and the seat is smoothed and flattened.

Carl shoves his door open. He swings out, his fingers hooked in the raingutters, and drops himself into the chair. "Better lock it. Just because it's your daddy's neighborhood—"

She punches the locks down.

Carl catches at the wheels as they move up the drive. Grace feels the pull, the slackened weight—the wheels skipping ahead in the gravel.

"Don't help me, Carl. Let me do it," she says.

Grace moves a few steps up the slope of the drive and quits. Her hair, crimped and brassy, falls against his shoulders. "I've got to rest," she tells him. "I've got to get some new shoes. This snow."

"What do you mean?" Carl says.

"The snow always soaks through my shoes."

Carl reaches down and pushes the wheels and she walks along behind the chair, not making a move to help him.

They pass under the lifted door of the garage, going along in the windowlight. They pass the push mower, the tools. The chair is gliding. There are racks of skis and fishing rods, a canoe hanging down from the rafters.

"Dad," Grace says.

"He can't hear you."

"How do you know?"

"Because he can't," Carl says.

Carl reaches up and slaps the window.

"Try the door," he tells her.

Helen, when she sees the car, doesn't know whose it is. She does not recognize the girl who steps out of it. There are photographs, of course, of all the girls, portraits that sat on the TV. But these have been in a drawer for some months now, almost since Helen moved in.

Helen has her own things, her own teacups to drink from, her own children to want to look at. But the house is full, you can hardly move.

She calls down the stairs to Walter. He must hear her, he must have heard the dogs. But he doesn't answer.

The door opens, and the girl walks in. She lifts the lid off the pot of potatoes Helen is boiling on the stove.

"Carl," the girl says and he says, "We got all night, so help me."

The girl is hauling the front wheels of the chair up the shallow step into the kitchen, her back turned to Helen as she comes down the stairs.

Carl says, "You must be the new wife."

"What did you say?" the girl says.

"I said you must be the new wife."

When the girl turns to look at Helen, Helen realizes who she is.

"And you must be Francesca," Helen says.

Helen holds her hand out.

"I'm the youngest."

"Of course you are. And you are?" Helen says to Carl.

"Carl," he says. "It's Grace."

He holds his hand out. He has broad, thick hands, a weak mouth. His sleeves are torn off at the shoulder seams.

"Pardon me?" Helen says.

"It ain't Francesca," Carl says. "It's Grace."

"This is Carl," Grace says. She smiles a little, wrinkling up her nose.

"Yeah," he says, "I said that."

"We should have called first. But we were out," Grace says, "we were driving around. I thought we'd just——"

"Stop by," says Carl, "you know."

"Well, what a nice surprise. May I take your coat?"

Helen holds out her hand to take Grace's coat.

"I ain't wearing a coat," Carl says.

"Then let me take your coat," Helen says again.

"My coat's all wet from the snow," Grace says.

She turns her back to Helen, works her coat down to her elbows, straightens her arms, steps out of it, as though she has rehearsed each move. "I don't have a good coat for the snow," she says. "It hardly ever snows, you know. These shoes—"

Carl pops his chair up on its back wheels and wheels himself out of the kitchen.

"He likes to look around."

Grace turns, too, lurches off. She walks on the bias, jerked, her head tipped, one shoulder dropped, weirdly stiff and listing.

That she walks off at all is what works at Helen; it is what Walter does, with not a word. You want to talk?—fall in, rake leaves, do whatever he is doing. Trail him from room to room.

The snow is melting, dripping from the hem of Grace's coat onto Helen's slippers. Helen checks the pockets, lumpy, filled—with butterscotch, scraps of string, wads of wadded tissue. Finders, she thinks, keepers, the whole tribe of them. She is living in a museum of somebody else's life.

She found packets of letters in Grace's drawers, sealed, bound with a rubberband, from a boy in Arizona: *Baby, where are you? I am not heard from you, baby, baby why?*

Saltines and vaginal sponges. Half a dozen splitting pairs of a dead grandmother's shoes.

Helen hangs Grace's coat on the back of a chair and follows her into the living room.

Walter is in his wingback, in his usual place at this time of the day, sitting facing the wall. He likes to sit there and listen to music. He has hung his wet coat on the arm of his chair, snagged his cap on the collar. Grace stops behind him.

"Hello, Daddy."

He nods and tells her to listen.

She kisses the top of his head.

"What is this?"

He touches his ear for Grace to listen.

"What is it? What are you listening to? What's he listening to?" she says.

Helen doesn't have a chance to answer—Carl is spinning into the room. He stops his chair in front of Walter's chair.

"This is Carl," Grace says.

"Carl," Walter says.

They lean together and shake hands.

"I didn't see no Jacuzzi," Carl says.

"What do you mean?" Walter says.

Carl looks at Grace.

"You said they had Jacuzzi. She told me you had Jacuzzi."

"No," Walter says.

"Goats?" Carl says. "Did you used to have you some goats?"

"Years ago," Walter says.

"Well, okay," Carl says, "that's something." He rocks his head some. "Yeah, that's something."

Carl steers himself around the room, his chair leaving tracks in the carpet—swirled spots where he tips and spins. He picks a vase up.

"You got yourself a real nice place, Dr. H. All right if I call you Dr. H, Dr. H? That suit you?"

Walter is quiet. He keeps an eye shut.

"You'll stay for dinner?" Helen asks.

She half sings it, a girly lilt that makes her sound drunk and cheerful.

"Is this your mother?" Carl says.

He holds a photograph up for Grace to see.

"There's plenty," Helen says.

She can pull out the ham from the back of the fridge, add flakes to the mashed potatoes. "There's always plenty. But you'll excuse me."

She pinches the flounce of her nightgown as though she is about to curtsy.

"I'll put some clothes on."

"Fine by me," Carl says. "Grace?"

"We should have called first," Grace says again.

"Hey, Grace?"

"Yeah," she says.

"You sure do look like your mother."

They don't go in right away when Helen calls them.

Grace stays in the room with her father, talking to the dogs through the sliding glass door. The dogs are whining, prancing, little light caps of snow on their heads. Grace licks the glass door—that's a doggie kiss—and one of the dogs licks back at her. She giggles.

She has an awful, wincing giggle. It is surprising—even to Walter.

But even this is not surprising, to be surprised. It is the order of the day, of the years she has lived. She has broken something, wandered off; she rode her bike through a plate glass door.

Months pass and not a peep and then, *voilà*, she appears again with some new affliction. She giggles and it sounds like choking. She sits on the floor and swallows and it sounds as though something living is being squeezed through her throat or sprung.

"Goddamnit," Walter says. "Get up, get up."

"It's on," Helen says. "It's dinner."

Walter gets up onto his legs first, pushes off his knees with his hands. He swings his chest up. Both of his hip joints catch and pop and his ankle wants to slip off his foot when he walks.

Carl glides in, takes his place at the table.

"You got to get your mind right, Doc. That's the whole trick," he says. He picks his fork up. "You get your mind wrapped around it. You got to. Me, I got no—"

"I haven't the vaguest idea," Walter says.

"Come on, man, I see you. It hurts you just to walk. Me," Carl says, "I got nothing. I got no pain, I got nothing. I really feel for you."

"You can shut up," Walter says.

"Don't," Grace says, "Daddy."

She walks around behind her father and hooks her arms around his chest. She lays her face against his neck and holds him.

"Naw, man, listen. Hey."

"You all sit," Helen says, and pours the wine, picks up the platter of ham. "In a minute, it won't be worth eating."

"What the hell do you want?" Walter says.

Carl picks up a glass, taps it against another glass.

"Here's to you, Doc."

Grace is whispering to her father. She kisses the collar of his shirt. She kisses along one shoulder seam, watching for him to speak.

"I love you too, honey," Walter says at last.

"Here's to love, then. To love," Carl says.

They take their places at the table.

Carl passes the bowl of potatoes to Grace. Grace's hands shake; her whole body shakes. She takes hold of the bowl from the bottom. It is hot. She jerks her hand back, knocks over a glass of wine.

"Pfoo," she says. "I didn't mean to."

Helen finds a towel, dabs at the wine.

"Well, how's everything?" Walter asks. "How's your new job, Francesca?"

"It ain't Francesca," Carl says, "it's Gracie. She changed her name to Grace."

"Did she."

Walter draws in his lips, puckers his chin.

"Nobody tells me anything. I'm always the last to know."

He shakes his napkin out.

"Do you like your job?" he asks her.

"What job is that?" Carl says.

"I like it fine," Grace says.

"Carl," she says.

"Goddamn. Goddamn, Grace. You kick me? You think I can't feel you kick me?

Carl jabs at the slice of ham on his plate, eats into a round on the spit of his fork.

"You don't want her at the VA anyway, Doc. A job like that. All them animals."

Carl serves himself more potatoes, makes a place with his spoon for the gravy to pool. The muscle knots up in his arm.

"Grace, pass me them beans, please."

She pushes the bowl across the table.

"Aren't you eating?" Walter asks her.

She picks her fork up.

"She don't eat," Carl says. "You got any bread? Sometimes she'll eat bread for supper."

Helen brings her two slices of bread on a plate.

"Butter?" Helen asks her.

"If you got it," Carl says.

Helen goes to the fridge for butter. Carl is eating the bread, watching her, her skirt pulling tight in places. He winks at Walter.

"You done all right."

"Listen, buddy."

Walter stands up.

"You want to fuck with me?"

Carl hops his chair out in front of Walter. He makes a little mocking charge that rattles the plates on the table.

"Yeah, boy, old man. Fuck with me. Please."

Walter stands there, blinking. He turns and walks out of the room.

Carl winks at Grace. "Give me that loaf," he says.

Grace goes to the counter, picks up the bread with both hands. She keeps an eye on the bread, walking with it, holding the loaf out in front of her, leans—as though she is making her way against wind.

"You got a real good girl, Dr. H," Carl says, loudly now. "Them guys at the VA liked her."

Walter puts on opera, sits down again in the wing back.

Helen tips a slice of bread from the loaf and puts it down in front of Grace. "Eat, now. You haven't eaten."

"I haven't eaten," Grace says.

"Mostly she keeps shit around, see. Likes to save it."

"Will you leave her alone?" Helen says.

"Leave her alone? Why, Mommy?"

Carl passes his hand in front of Helen's face.

"Open your eyes, please."

Walter swings the door shut between them. A little quiet— why not? Is it so much to ask?

"You people," Carl says.

He pops a wheelie, knocks his legs into the table. "You're starting to get to me. Whyn't you talk to me?"

Helen sits with her mouth pressed closed. Grace tears at the soft middle dough of the bread, rolls a ball in the palms of her hands.

"Gracie, okay, I got it," Carl says. "I seen her a mile away. She's fucked. I understand that. But, you, cupcake, and the doctor,

you confuse me. Because you look okay! No kidding. You look more
or less all there."

He pulls a finger through the mashed potatoes.

"Okay, so a person can fool you. Even Gracie could fool
you, pretty as she is, if she don't say much, if you don't really see
her move. Say if you saw a picture—woo. She's a looker, our Gracie, don't you think so?"

He licks his finger, holds the lump of potato in his mouth
as he talks.

"I carry three shots of her in my wallet, see, just to say, Look
here. This here is the one that Doc took. That's Brenja," Carl says,
and points to the dog. "I guess he's the one that names the dogs."

He holds the photograph out for Helen to see: Grace is
three, maybe four, lying barebottomed along the dog, watching it
nurse its puppies.

"I just love that," Carl says.

He tucks the photo away, slides another one out.

"This one I took."

Grace is lying in a fog in a field of cows in the photograph
that Carl took, her skin pale as snow, hair a tangle, a clump of
grass in her mouth.

"She's a doozie," Carl says, "don't you think so? Here she is
a baby, little fat thing, little tub of butter. Hardly moved, I guess—
he must of told you. Hardly made a sound. But you can't see that
from a picture, you can't tell. Keep your distance, that's the trick.
Keep a picture. But you know that, I see. Because Grace isn't even
yours, right? Your kids were born okay, I guess. That's lucky. Grew
up, moved away. The rest of his bunch too—doctors, lawyers,
whatnot. Not a peep from them, they been busy. It's good to keep
busy, don't you think? Don't you think so, Gracie girl?"

"Oh, yes," Grace says.

"Take Mommy. Bet you she stays real busy—charity work,
blood drives, Meals on Wheels, all that. Am I right?" Carl says.

Grace tips up her plate to show Carl the face, the crooked, zagging mouth she has made on the rim with the dough.

"You got a way with food, baby."

Carl takes a ball of dough from her plate, a dingy, misshapen eye, tosses it, catches it in his mouth.

"You got to watch her all the time. I go into her room at the Y one time—she's got stashes, plates underneath the bed. She's got food in the drawer with her underpants. It's nasty, man, maggots, mold and shit, so help me. I don't get it, okay, I admit that. But I don't just go *eew*."

He holds up his glass for Helen to fill; she fills it, the wine sloshing out, Carl rocking himself in his chair. Then he spins away from the table, slams into a door—it flaps open. He pushes through. The dogs are outside, barking, mouths hazing the glass porch door. He flies a kiss at the dogs as he passes. Flies a kiss at Walter. Makes a lap: living room, darkened hall, then the wheels of his chair are stuttering over the polished tile of the kitchen.

"I'm the man with the news, Mommy!"

Helen covers her face with her hands.

"Don't be like that."

He yanks his chair to a stop.

"It ain't Gracie's fault. Didn't get enough air at birth, okay. Whatever. It happens. She can't do things, she tries. I think she tries. But you can't just leave her alone, Mommy! That's stupid."

He is knocking into Helen's chair.

"Take your hands off."

He pulls her hands from her face.

He says, "Look at me. Look, look. How'd you like to be our Gracie? Look to me for love, man?"

He jams his fingers between Helen's knees.

"No kidding. Bitter fucking cripple. You got you a job at the VA scrubbing cripples' potties. How'd you like that? It's a pleasure. Satisfying, too. But, hey, whoa, hold up, you know all about it. You got orphans, refugees, twisters coming through. I got ears, okay, I hear it. Ladies-Something-Something-for-the-Blah-Blah-Blah. You ladies—riding around on your cunts like that. So pretty so, oh god," he is scratching runs in her nylons. "You should of come and seen her, Mommy. It of lifted your heart, I swear it."

It is phosphorous the wisteria needs—but Walter should have done that in October. You thatch the grass in April, after the tulips have dropped their blooms.

He keeps his good eye shut, Walter does, sitting there, beginning to see again with the other eye as with an aperture being opened. As it opens, what he hears seems to brighten. The wing back, given the wings and the way he sits, makes it easy, with the music loud, to hear only the music, little more, and to watch the snow keep falling. But then the dogs start: Carl is sailing through the room in his chair.

Walter goes to the door to hush the dogs and he sees, he thinks, that they have found the bird he lobbed into the trees. He slides the door open. One of the dogs trots off with the bird and stands with it in the snow coming down beyond where the porch light reaches. Walter calls to the dog. It lies down, lays its head in the snow with the bird in its mouth between its outstretched paws.

Walter says, "Stay," and moves toward it. The dog moves off. Walter shows it the broom he keeps near the door to keep the dogs out of the garden, to keep them from digging the lawn up, to hush them when they bark.

His daughter taps on the glass behind him.

"What happened?" she wants to know.

Walter swings the broom up on his shoulder.

"Come on and help me," he says.

Grace follows her father out over the yard, crouching, as he does, trailing the dog through the snow. The air is warmer, velvety; a fog has drifted in.

Thd dog has a squirrel, not a bird, Walter sees that now. He strikes the ground with his broom.

"Goddamnit," he says. "Stay. I said stay."

The dog skulks off. Helen makes it out as far as the porch and stops as quick as she sees him—this silent creature she married, stalking a dog with his girl.

Carl locks the glass door behind her. When she turns around, he waves. He flips the outside light off.

"Walter, please," Helen cries. She starts toward him. "I can't see you."

Grace takes her by the hand.

"Over here," she says. "He's not far."

And he's not. He is waiting for Helen, his arms at his sides. His house is going dark. He lets his wife stand on his feet, on the tops of his boots, perches his hands on the small of her back.

"Get them out of here," she whispers.

Something is funny, wrong, to Helen, too solid as she presses against him. He's aroused, she thinks, and blurts out a laugh. She fumbles at the crotch of his trousers, finds a hard, distended mass.

"What in the world?" she asks him.

Walter is grinning. She can't see this—there are so few lights left on. He pulls a golf ball from his pocket, bends her fingers around it.

"You've been golfing?" she says.

"Not exactly."

"Not exactly?" Helen says. "What can that mean?"

She twists away from him.

"She's not my daughter," Helen says.

And not, Walter thinks, he has thought it before—she is not his daughter, either. Not his doing, at any rate. An accident, damage at birth—nothing he passed down.

His wife is walking away up the slope to the house, Grace falling in behind her. Helen steps out of one of her shoes—the sharp heel sunk, snagged in the grass—and she pitches, slowly, forward, coming down on her hip in the snow.

"In all my life," she says. "Your father."

"Your poor feet," Grace says. "You need shoes."

Grace slips the shoe free—it is like dragging a root from soft ground.

"We had a farm," she says. "Did he tell you? Horses and billy goats. And when I was born Daddy planted trees up and down both sides of the drive."

"He's a busy man," Helen says.

"And the trees grew faster than I did, one right across from the other and such, all up and down the drive."

Room by room, Carl rolls through the house, switching the intercoms on. He leaves traces: a spatter of piss on the toilet seat, a spoon in the disposal. The cheesecake he finds at the back of the fridge, he probes and strokes with his thumb. He folds a bed back; he turns a TV upside down.

He searches their drawers, their closets, swipes a flaking snapshot he finds of Grace's mother, blurred—a girl in a boat on the ocean. He swipes a cheap loop of pearls and a stocking—sleek things for his pockets. For his window, he takes a delicate carving of an animal he cannot name.

When the telephone rings he picks it up, gasps into the mouthpiece. When he breathes into the intercom, the sound travels through every room.

"Halloo, halloo. Carl here."

Grace nickers: she had forgotten: there are intercoms inside and out. Her father had insisted on it—all those speakers when her mother was sick, everything pinched and glinty.

She walks off the porch and, squatting, tamps out her name with the flat of her hand in the unbroken glaze of snow. She writes *Grace* then scuttles in a squat to a new patch and tamps out F-R-A-N.

Her father is coming to her, dragging his foot in the snow.

He had made rounds through the house when his wife was sick, turning the speakers up. Spoke to Sarah, when he spoke at all, from the porch, the garage, the living room. And if his wife was speaking that day, from whatever place she had dreamed herself to, from the farm, from the shabby flat in New Orleans, she asked: *Walter, where are you?*

On the verandah, he would tell her, conceding.

Verandah. Carport. Parlor.

On the verandah: the blue sizzle of the buglight—he insisted—always on. There was not a closet, a corner, an hour left where you could go and not have to hear her—every howl, every sip and fidget. You could forget almost to breathe—the whole of the house seemed to do it.

The dog, loping out in front of her father, reaches Gracie first, drops the squirrel on its back beside her. Grace goes to her knees to see it. The squirrel's mouth is still pulsing; its small legs are canted out, its paws drawn up like spiders. The white strip of its belly is mounded and soft, the broadly gaping seam of an animal stuffed with cotton. Grace nudges the tail and it flickers. She prods the ribs; the body curls and spits.

"What are you doing?" her father says.

"I'm thinking."

"Can't you think standing up with the rest of us?"

Grace turns up the cuffs of her father's pants.

"I'm thinking."

She pulls the wrinkle from the neck of his sock.

He steps away from her.

"Francesca," Walter says.

He could weep almost, done in by her name. All her long life he had said it.

She taps the squirrel's head and it hisses.

"Don't do that."

"It's not dead yet," she says.

"I can see."

When she reaches to touch the squirrel again, Walter hauls her to her feet by her elbow. She stumbles into him.

"You don't listen," Walter says.

He bends to knock the folds from his cuffs. "You just do your own thing."

"*I'm* listening, Doc," Carl says from inside the house, a broadcast over the intercom. "I can see. You okay, Gracie girl?"

Grace sniffles. She hooks a thumb in each ear not to hear him.

"I took her out to Pop's place one time, it's in the country."

Grace hums a song, makes it up, walks away off to the bank of trees.

"He's got animals and all like that. Keeps a garden. I thought she'd like that. We do a little this and that for Pop, give him a boost, he's old. I'm talking nothing—a weed here and there, maybe sweep something out. Maybe it takes half the morning. Gracie disappears. Does her own thing, I heard that. And me and Pop, we're neither of us, we can't go and find her. I got a kid brother—I think *he* could go, but he is gone off, too. The two of them—disappeared. You get the picture. He's a pretty boy, handpainted. Never been busted up."

Helen slumps onto the picnic bench. She is tired; she has been tired for years.

And the day began so sleepily, sweetly, reading a book on the fold-out while the snow kept on in the gauzy light tilting, spinning down. She heard tinkering, nothing more—and now this, and there would be more of this, she knows. Chin up, carry on, count your lucky blessings. My.

She bends her leg up, examines the run in her nylons. The skin underneath is frayed. *Fine,* Helen thinks. It gives her something to show to Walter, how he walks off: *Look what our dinner guest did.*

"Here's what I thought," Carl says over the intercom.

He has rolled his chair into the bathroom.

"I was thinking you could spare us some dough, man. We got hospital bills, you know that."

"We have bills of our own," Walter says.

"Our own?" Carl says. "What does that mean? What the fuck does that mean?"

"Walter," Helen says and pets his arm, "be quiet."

A light comes on in the bathroom and Carl's face appears in the window, mashed against the glass; his nose, bent—two holes; his lips flexing, stiffening, then flowering out obscenely.

Walter pitches the golf balls at Carl, which rocket away off the glass.

"Don't be stupid," Helen says, and she jostles the door to their bedroom.

"You want in, Mommy?"

"Don't call me that."

"There's plenty. I'm checking out the doctor's medicine chest: two of them, three of that, once a day as needed. Good God, Doc. You're a walking toxic event."

He runs water.

"I'm own take a few. Just a tickle," Carl says, "see what happens. I'm give out. I been rolling all over the house, man. You got

ROOMS. Some I can't even get to."

He shakes some pills out. "A little help here and there. Why not? We got ER bills, we got ambulance. Gracie, tell them about the ambulance."

He turns the faucet off. "Hey, Grace?"

Grace is down by the dog house kicking around through the leaves.

"She gets bit by a ant, she stubs her toe, and she calls the goddamn—"

"She didn't used to," Walter says.

"The hell she didn't. She calls the goddamn ambulance. Grace! Where'd she go, Doc? Ain't you watching her?"

They hear him coming. He bashes out onto the porch.

"I oughta knock your goddamn teeth down your throat. Grace! Gracie girl."

Carl rolls up close to the railing, lifts himself out by the arms of his chair to see across the yard.

"So help me, man."

He cannot see her, cannot get to her—it is steps going off the porch. There is a hot wire strung to keep the dogs away below the wooden railing.

Walter pokes his nose up, sniffs at the air. He starts toward the patch of pine trees and, seeing nothing of smoke or flame, turns, breaks into a clumsy trot. It is inside the house, it must be.

But it's not: it is the scorch of Carl's pantleg he smells against the wire fence, and the stink of flesh searing.

Carl slams back into the picnic bench, swatting at his pants.

Helen sinks to her knees in her nursey way and hitches the cloth up his calf. She fingers the burn and, gently, gravely, his boot heel clamped between her knees, applies a compress of snow.

"Who, Mommy," Carl brays, laughing. "That's the first thing I felt in yeeears."

There are two kennels built of chainlink at the boundary of the yard, a doghouse in each, an automatic feeder. The floor of each kennel is so deep in shit you have to walk on your tiptoes to keep it from welting over your shoes. That's what Grace does—she walks on tiptoes, crawls into the doghouse.

They cannot see her in there. She doesn't answer Carl when he calls.

Helen wrestles the wheelchair down the steps, bumps it over the walkway.

The windowlight flutters on—Walter is on his rounds. Lights on, speakers off. He toddles from room to room, seeking damage, surveying what is his.

Helen comes upon the ladder at the far end of the house, leaned up against the gutter. She kicks off her shoes and goes up—quickly, tottering on her arches, over the icy rungs. Grace is up there, she thinks, she must be, blundering over the shingles.

Helen feels brave and suddenly useful. She can do this for years to come—clamber onto rooftops, venture out in the dark and snow. A great weakening surge of something bristles her arms and legs.

Grace watches all this from the dog house—how Helen bobbles up, hooks a toe. Then she is gone, crept out onto the pitch in the dark.

There is Carl, still, and the sheepdog to watch, the sheep-dog circling Carl, snapping at the wheels of his chair. There is the milky beam from the lighthouse, the hum of the turning bulb.

The sheepdog rushes at Carl. He flies it back with his elbow.

Carl hunkers, his chin tucked, snarls, spinning his chair as the dog moves, keeping the dog out in front of him, taunting, he is like that, and Grace sees—she is standing now, tiptoeing out to help him—the orbs of mud his chair plows up and hears, sometimes, her name.

She whistles. It will come to her—the sheepdog's name.

And the light from over the golf course, that will come to her, too. You simply stand just so and wait for it: a beacon, a sweeping pulse, convincing, the light triggered by dark, by weather: needed, that's the idea.

Nothing is missing, nothing damaged. No bedcover browned by flame.

Walter stands for a time in the doorway of the room that used to be, that would be again—it wasn't his idea—Francesca's. *Francesca's*—he would insist on that. There were Francescas all through his side of the family, every dead generation.

A few of her things are still here—figurines of horses, a family of porcelain dolls.

Down the hall a short stretch is their bedroom—his and Sarah's, his and Helen's. Walter tries to remember what it felt like to him to be lonely—before Helen, when he was alone.

He has drawers full of places to go. Rivers to fish, famous creeks.

Old age would come upon him in his hip boots.

He pulls the door shut.

The hospitals, the phone calls from distant precincts, all of it, mucking around with lowlifes—it is already back in his hands. She will steal from them. She will drive their cars into lamp posts. She will break her neck at the square dance, lift her skirts for the guards at the gate—for the men you have to check in with before you are allowed to go home.

coquina

I was to marry him. I had no doubt of it. But I saw easily that it mattered to him that I take no notice of his plan.

It was not like him, it was strange of him—to have brought us at all to the island. He had secured a room in the island hotel, a clean place of thickest coquina, the tide gnawing at its heels.

The room, the entire island, even the sea seemed to quiet. He had consulted the gods, I decided. And this unnerved him, it surprised him, I saw, how the moment embarked upon in such quiet came to swagger before us and leer.

We saw no automobiles. We saw none but the crudest wobbling ways for the few mewling carts to run on. No bridge stretched over the inlet; the natives bullied their way by foot as they must, to market, to the city from which we had travelled and to which, bound anew by a mulish faith, we would return to make our home. They went weakly, carting their old in the ebb tide over the oyster beds.

The trip was pleasing, the passage by ferry from the mainland we made over the open sea. The night was soft and damply mooned. He suggested that, once we had settled, we walk; we would take in the night's salt breeze.

I agreed, happily. I meant no trouble to him.

As we walked, I saw he allowed the box to drop to his feet in the sand. I saw the broad spotted face of a pony as we walked—there were bands of feral ponies—peering out from the bearded trees. The sand was fine and polished. I swung my foot, as we went, through the ruffle of foam—that we might know where we had lingered, that we might, in turning, easily see where perhaps the box had been.

I confess this much surprised me, it worried me, that he had tossed the box onto the sand. I said nothing; I had decided. He had considered the hazard himself, understand. He is careful, it is his habit; he is thorough, such a man. He would make no failing gesture.

And yet I worried. I thought how easily the box might coast out. They would find it among the oysters beds, some child at her game, some luckie.

It was nothing. The loss of the ring would be nothing. It was his disappointment I dreaded, supposing the plan went askew.

We walked on. I understood I was meant to discover the ring when we had turned to return to our quarters. I saw my surprise, my elation; I imagined, as a kind of practice, that my voice might thicken with joy.

I understood, I believe, the custom well enough—my part in it, and his. I recognized the artifacts, the necessary gestures. He would fall to one knee, as is the custom.

I understood that the box would be velvet, it is velvet, I need not explain. The lid is jointed—that I might, as I wish, snap it shut, that he might stand it open.

I saw him kneeling, a plain man, decent, mine, the small box sprung in his hand.

He spun round; he lurched past me, I was walking some distance behind him, poor man. He sank to both knees pitifully and begin to claw at the sand.

The ring was plain, it is plain, this is his habit.

And yet to see it surprised me. I found myself giddy, I was gladdened—to snug it over my knuckle. The long ardor, the looseness of girlhood at an end.

We kissed lightly; we brushed the sand from our knees. The light of our room fell toward us as we went, happily, in our languor; it swam to us from the shadows swung out of the bearded trees.

I meant no trouble to him.

I mean no trouble now.

That we were greeted at the door—this is the custom, is it not? And it is, is it not, the custom to boast, to say, *Look*, was it not, *what has happened?*

Besides, I found I wished to hear it—how lovely, such a ring, how lucky for me. I felt luckier still to hear it.

The night was strange to me, it was pleasing, the sea, the sweet wide faces of the ponies as we went, showing themselves in the trees. I was dizzy with it, I was foolish, I suppose, I who so terribly seldom felt—undone—even then, so very timid I was, I was—watchful of him, let me say it—you! Say, *Watchful, kind. She was careful,* say. *She bore him three seemly girls.*

The clerk said, "Isn't that perfectly lovely."

And I felt it, it had a way in me—the stone in my throat, the habit of love.

He was in a fury when we reached the room.

The clerk would come to us in the night, he was convinced, with a potion, a bludgeon—what would prevent her?—a blade. She would plunge an ax into his skull.

Could I not see how easily?

How stupid I had been to boast?

No ferry at such an hour, a fog sweeping in.

What hours, what years he had labored and saved—to have it come to this.

"To this!"—he was trembling, and shook me.

She would set him adrift in the sea.

Impossible—that I might calm him. He could see no means of escape. Was he to tie his trousers around my neck, cart me over the oyster beds, reckon a course by the stars?

I saw myself slung across a pony, drenched, my dark hair drifting prettily and fouling in the weeds.

She was a clerk, understand, paid to greet us, paid to sort out keys. She was nothing to me, a service to me, I had scarcely seen her.

But he had seen her. He spoke of patches of yellow where her scalp showed through—she had cut her hair like a boy's. The skin had split on her knuckles and bled. And she had bitten herself—bitten herself!—and what in God's name would I say to that, how did I mean to explain away that—the deep print he had seen in her arm?

I saw her clearly then. She would swim him beyond the breakwater away from the windward shore. I saw his arms swinging gently from their sockets, the mound of his back above the sea. The surfers would arrive by morning—careless, brown-limbed boys mounted on their boards. They would not see him. They would lay him cleanly open with their fins.

It was only the ring she would covet at first. But give her time, give her leisure. Who would there be to stop her, with him bobbing in the sea?

She would make me her pet, her kin, quick to shame, obedient, her creature, the bones parting in my knees.

He drew the knot of rope from his satchel and, with this, lashed the door to the bed to the stop to the sink and back to the massive bureau. He lashed the window shut. He fashioned a rattle of the shells we had found to hang from the door should she shake it.

I did not think that she would shake it.

A night clerk, a girl.

I slept. The air, the sea, I had no trouble sleeping.

In sleep I built him a crown of nails. The nails were mildewed. We could push them home with our hands.

Such a man as he.

I waked to find him. He sat in the chair in his shabby briefs and picked at his cheek, at his knees. He crossed his legs at the knees and the ankles—twice.

And this surprised me.

Old captain, mine, old suffering school.

In such a way the night passed, in such a way the years.

someone is always missing

The baby was sleeping. The sisters had gone to the garden. There was flagstone around the garden. Lemon thyme bunched up between the slabs of stone. The dog lay down in the shade in the thyme and watched the girls in the garden.

The older sister said, "Listen for the baby, big dog."

It was the older sister's baby. It was the older sister's dog, the older sister's garden, beside the older sister's house. The house was built in the sage and pine that grew on the slope of a hogback that tilted out of the plains. You could see across the plains from the garden.

"And these," the younger sister said, "are these keepers?"

The older sister, Libby, nodded. She knelt on the flagstone and pointed.

It had been an easy birth. But it was hard still, bending. It was still hard for Libby to get herself around. "That's heartsease," she said, pointing. "There's motherwort and feverfew. This is hound's-tongue, here; rue. The rest of this is garbage."

The beds were dusty. The dust that lifted away from the plains and the chalky dust of the concrete plant coated each leaf and bloom. The sisters knocked the dust off as they weeded; they heaped the weeds on the slabs of stone that Libby's husband had lain around the garden.

"I'm glad you came," Libby said to her sister.

The younger sister was Rose. She was the taller, the prettier one. She was the one their father kept moving from school to school. "Did you hear that?" Rose asked.

"What is it?"

"I thought I heard the baby."

Libby stopped and listened. She heard the wind moving the limbs of the trees and the dog, when it let its mouth drop open, breathing. But she could not hear the baby.

"Will Daddy come see the baby?" Rose asked.

"He says so. As soon as he can."

Rose's shorts worked up as she weeded until her underpants showed, the elastic slack and useless. There were dusty streaks on the back of her shorts where she had wiped her hands.

"I mean it," Libby said. "I really am glad you came. It helps me. With the baby and all."

The dog rolled onto its back in the thyme. It showed the girls its body.

The days were growing hotter. The snowmelt was over, the runoff not plunging out of the mountains anymore.

The sisters moved on into the flowerbeds, into the bed where the iris was blooming. They had planted the iris the year before, not long after Libby married, before the baby had begun to show. It was a year winter came all at once. The girls had dug the new bed with a mattock in the falling snow, guessing at the borders of the older beds, the wasted leaves from the older bulbs the iris would bloom among. The iris had grown straight and healthily, sending up tall, sturdy stems whose blooms—this was why the sisters were digging them up now—were a murky, riverish brown.

Rose chipped the dirt up, twisted her spade to pry up the roots. "I'm so thirsty," she said. "All this digging."

"We'll be finished soon," Libby said. "If we go in, we'll wake the baby."

Rose dropped her spade. She walked to the hose, turned the faucet open and drank until the water that had been left in the hose and been warmed by the sun ran out. She let the water, running cold, run out into the iris bed to make the bed easier to dig in.

"You can't do that," Libby said. "They won't let you water when it's dry like this."

"Who is *they* ?" Rose said.

"You know."

Rose turned off the faucet. She knelt again in the iris bed. "You know why *they* bring flowers to the hospital?" she said.

"Should I?" her sister said.

"Because then they don't have to smell you."

Rose leaned into the stand of blooms. She dipped her nose among the petals of one of the blooms, the crest and beardless falls.

It had always amazed her—that things knew when to grow. *All those months in the ground in the snow*, she thought, and she remembered the snow of the year before suddenly, earnestly falling. Rose had been between schools that year, their father going from job to job.

It was their father who had sent her out. He sent her to Libby with a dachshund, which Libby gave away, and with a shopping bag full of rhizomes which he guessed, in his note, were tulips. *At the very least,* the note read, *these should keep your sister out of harm's way.*

Libby said, "They teach you that in school, I guess."

"I guess so."

Rose tossed a muddy clump she had pulled free onto the heap of weeds on the flagstone. Libby squatted behind her. She picked the iris up by the handful, and the weeds, loading her arms from the top of the pile. She saw the nubs of Rose's spine underneath her shirt, poked out from her curving back. Rose was thin, thinner than Libby had seen her get, boyish and hard. Libby, this soon after the baby, felt thick and slow and swelled still. She squatted until her knees hurt and stood up slowly behind her sister and said to the back of her head, "You didn't have to go through with it. Nobody made you."

"You would know, of course."

"I'm just saying, Rose."

Rose went on digging. "You know what's funny?" Rose said to her sister. "They don't even have to talk to you. They just stand around near the door."

She swiped at her mouth with the sleeve of her shirt. "They took turns," she said. "When Jack got tired, Daddy came limping up the hall. Don't you think that's funny?"

"And what did they say?" Libby said.

"Nothing. They just stood there. I was in bed, reading, filing my nails, whatever, and I would hear them. Jack came over every day. I kept thinking he would give up and say something, or that Daddy would—a word, my name, whatever. One of them or the other. I thought once that maybe one of them would come in and sit on the bed. God."

She jabbed around in the hole she had dug with the dented nose of her spade.

"They must have said something," Libby said.

"Sure, like, 'Honey, it's nothing.' Something like that?" Rose said.

"Forget it."

"'All they have to do is go up in there and squirt a bit—'"

"I said forget it," Libby said.

"I mean weeks of it. God," she said. "Them standing around in the hall out there eating gingersnaps." Rose looked up at her sister. She saw her sister not seeing her, not looking. "Don't you see?" she said.

"Not really."

"Really?" Rose insisted.

"I don't. I don't understand you. I don't see why you had to wait so long so you had to even go to the hospital and actually have to *have* the thing." She was walking across the flagstone. "It's unreasonable. It's just a lot of moaning."

Libby walked around behind the house. She dropped the armload of iris and weeds on the heap of limbs and clippings and scratched around on a head of a dog who followed wherever she went now and was standing at her knee. She listened for the baby. She climbed onto a stack of concrete blocks and looked through the high window. The baby was still asleep. The dog was standing behind Libby, whining, ready to spring up onto the blocks. Rose was calling the dog from the garden. The telephone was ringing. Libby listened for Rose to go into the house and wake up the baby to answer the phone. But the phone kept ringing. Rose kept calling the dog from the garden. Libby watched the baby until the ringing stopped. The baby was still asleep when it stopped.

When Libby came back to the garden, Rose said, "That was Jack, I guess."

"What makes you say so?"

"Because I know him," Rose said. "He was calling to make sure I got here. He always does that."

"Well, that's good," Libby said.

"Do you think so?"

"Rose."

"He called the hospital, too. Isn't that good? He sent a big bunch of flowers."

Libby went back to digging, piling up the iris. A cluster of low, unimpressive clouds was being blown across the plains. A truck turned off the asphalt road and began to throw, from the slope of sage, a powdery veil of dust.

"Ah," Rose said, "the man of the house."

She walked out onto the driveway and waved at him as he came.

Libby threw together an easy meal while her husband played with the baby. He passed brightly colored rings above the baby's face, nudgled it under its chin. The baby's eyes were barely open. Its skull was still a funny shape, squeezed into a pointy hump at the top of the baby's head.

Libby's husband put the baby in a wicker basket and he set the basket on the floor at his feet when it was time to come to the table. The dog lay down near the basket, watching the baby, lifting up its head from between its paws whenever the baby moved at all or made the slightest sound.

"What a good dog," Rose said.

It lifted its head to let her pat it.

Libby's husband ate without speaking. When Rose twisted around to re-tie the robe she had come to dinner in, Libby's husband kept his eyes on his plate. When he had finished eating all the food on his plate, he picked the plate up and licked it, and when he put the plate down again, there were pieces of food in his beard. He had a sprawling, sunburnt beard and a lumpy, porous nose. His mouth was completely grown over. When he spoke to the baby, all they saw of his mouth was a neat row of tiny teeth and the tip of his tongue between them.

"Bloawgh," he said, "goochy goo. Talk to Big Bear, Baby."

He rocked the basket roughly and the baby sloshed side to side.

"Go easy," Libby told him.

The baby had to wear a harness—webbing and Velcro, shoulder to toe—to brace its leg. The leg had caught on something, some bone or cord or who knew what; it had been twisted around and broken in Libby long before the baby was born. The tendons and ligaments of the knee were torn so that the leg, the foot—it was better now, Libby knew it was getting better—but it was still something to see, the way it flopped around when the harness was off. With the harness off, the leg looked detachable, like the limb of a plastic doll.

Libby cleared the table. She came around behind her husband and knocked bits of food from his beard.

Rose brushed the dander from his shirt sleeve. The dog got up, whining, and walked underneath the table. Rose listened to it sniffing. It rubbed against her leg. She unwrapped the piece of chewed-up meat she had spat out into her napkin and held the meat in her hand.

"You better quit that," Libby's husband said. "I asked her not to do that."

"Do what?" Libby said.

Libby's husband kicked at the dog underneath the table.

"I'm just sitting here," Rose said.

"You're not," said the husband. "Goddamnit. I asked you not to do that."

"Do what?" Libby said.

Rose pushed away from the table. She held the meat out between the slats of her chair where the dog could see it behind her. The dog took a step, slowly, as though stepping hurt its paws. It was looking up at the husband.

"Do you want that?" the husband said to the dog.

Rose dropped the meat into the pocket of her robe.

The husband stood up.

"You want that?"

The dog sat down behind Rose's chair, pretending to be yawning.

"I thought so," the husband said.

"That's a good dog," he said, and walked over to the dog to pat it. He walked to the basket, the baby in the basket, and he carried it away from the table.

"Here you go," he said to his wife.

Libby saw, from his eyes, that he was grinning, and from his ears, which had moved a little way up the sides of his head.

He went out of the house with a hammer and saw, and with nails poking out of his pockets. He cut a few boards for the soffit, and stepped up the ladder with one of the boards and with nails sticking out of his mouth. He held the board against the joists with his shoulder.

Swallows built nests in the eaves. Clots of mud from the nests they built were spattered against the side of the house; mud was dried on the screens of the windows.

When he banged on the house, the dog barked.

Rose broke a glass on the faucet. She picked the pieces up, dropped them into the bottom of the glass, dropped the glass in the garbage. She rinsed the sink out, and filled it up again.

The wind was quitting. The boat was bottom-up in the yard.

Libby turned the water on in the bathroom. The dog went into the bathroom and lapped water from the toilet bowl.

Rose didn't wash the husband's—she did not wash Big Bear's plate. Instead, she wiped off the flowery rim where Big Bear had not quite licked it clean and she set the plate down in the dish rack. The rest of the plates, she scraped and stacked and left in the soapy water. Rose walked down the hall to the bathroom. The dog was curled up on the bathmat.

Libby took her clothes off. She took the baby's little jump-suit off, the baby's pilly harness. The baby's skin was chaffed underneath the harness, and flaking. Libby scraped off some of the flaked-up skin with the squarish nail of her thumb. She shut the faucet off and stepped into the tub, holding the baby against her. Its thin, bowed legs, when she sat down, hung between Libby's legs. She dipped the baby into the water.

Rose swung the top down on the toilet bowl and sat on it to watch. She scratched behind the dog's ears as she watched. The mirror rattled, and little ripples came up in the water in the tub whenever Big Bear drove a nail into the eaves with his hammer. He was working his way toward the bathroom, stopping to cut the soffit boards and then hitting in nails again.

"Here," Rose said, "I can help you."

Rose washed her sister's back for her, soaping it up and rinsing it with a cup she had brought from the kitchen.

Her sister's skin had gotten smoother. Libby's hair had gotten thicker, shinier than it used to be. Her breasts were bigger than Rose's now.

Rose slipped her hand under her sister's arm, turning the soap in her armpit. She moved the soap over her sister's ribs, which used to show underneath her skin. Libby lifted the baby away from her chest and held it propped against her legs, holding her arms away from her sides to let her sister wash her. Rose soaped up Libby's belly, her breasts, her nipples split and raw. She pushed into a nipple with the ball of her thumb. A little milk came out.

Libby felt her sister's hands shake.

"Rose, Rose," Libby said.

Rose had started very quietly crying. "I kept on letting the days pass so I could feel it move," she said. "I wanted to feel it, what that feels like. I know it's stupid."

Libby kissed her sister's fingertips. She handed her sister the baby.

Libby let Rose wash the baby—its bottom, its skinny legs, its little curling feet. She let Rose lather the dark hair whorled on the baby's funny head, Rose keeping the soap away from its face the way Libby had shown her. The baby jerked its little arms around. It poked out the little white callus on its lip it already had from sucking.

"Look," Libby said. "She likes it."

She stepped out of the tub to give them room to move and pulled a towel off the towel rack.

Libby's husband ran a saw through a board. He stepped up onto the ladder. With the claw of his hammer, he scraped at the mud that was left of the nests the swallows made.

Libby swung her hair up over her head to dry it.

Rose dipped the baby's head into the water. She turned the baby onto its belly, held it there, let go. The dog got up, barking. The baby started to swim. Only its little bottom, and the misshapen plate at the back of its head, stuck up out of the water. The baby lunged—jerky, froggish—paused, trailing its little crooked leg; it swam over half the length of the tub before Libby saw what her sister had done and knocked past her, screaming, and snatched the baby out of the water.

"What are you doing?" Libby screamed. She held the baby against her. The baby was quiet. She hit her sister across the mouth. "What did you think you were doing?"

"She was swimming," Rose said. "She liked it."

It was true that the baby was quiet. Its little mouth was open, it was waving its little hands—a baby newly enough from the womb that it could still do that, hold its breath and swim like that. It had not forgotten yet how to do that.

When it was dark outside and the wind had quit and the baby was in its crib asleep, Libby's husband came in. Rose heard him, big as he was, walk down the hall with his toolbox.

She tried to get the dog to sleep with her, tried to trap it underneath the covers. Rose patted the sheet, and tugged on the dog's collar, but the dog, when it jumped on the bed, only jumped right off again. She gave up. She swung the door shut to keep the dog in her room, and flipped the light off.

The beds—the one that Rose was in, and the one where Libby and her husband slept—were side by side, pushed against opposite sides of the wall. Rose listened for them through the plaster. She waited until they were quiet, until Libby and her husband seemed to be asleep, and then she went in to look at the baby. The baby was sleeping. It was making little sleeping sounds. The dog sat beside Rose and whimpered.

She went into the kitchen. She got Big Bear's plate from the dish rack and toasted four frozen waffles, heaped them with ice cream and chocolate sauce and ate them in the dark in bed. She let the dog lick the plate when she had finished. This time, when she patted the covers, the dog jumped up in the bed.

She dreamed: they were with the dog, she and Libby, among the mountains. There was snow still, in patches, and moss that grew over their knees. In the snow was an overturned pickup truck she and Libby climbed out of. Their clothes were torn. They looked for wounds, for broken bones. They found the baby—not Libby's baby, but the tiny thing that Rose felt drop into the toilet in the hospital—beginning to grow on her tongue.

Rose waked, and Libby and the dog and the baby waked, all at once before the sun: Big Bear had burned his toast. The dog got up. Rose lay in bed, listening, remembering she had turned the toaster to High to toast her frozen Eggos. She pulled her robe on, and let the dog out. She stood in the doorway, watching, in the light from the house, the dog following its nose.

It was dark still; the wind had not started to blow. Smoke was rising in columns from the concrete plant and drifting out over the plains, over a band of cottonwoods bent over a path of stones that had once been the bed of a river.

The boat was gleaming, bottom-up in the grass in the yard.

Rose tried to remember her dream. She remembered, instead, that she walked in her sleep for years before she moved from home, when home was a lush, dampened place, a county of hills and fences. In her sleep, she buried her family's shoes in the sawdust pile beside the barn. She waked herself in shopping malls, on roadways, in neighbors' yards—in places, some nights, she had never been and did not know how to go home from.

One night she waked, lying in a dew, in grass so tall she saw only leaves, threaded and sharp, and limpid stems, nodding their glossy heads. Something was eating toward her: she had fallen asleep in a field of cows. When a few of them found her, others came. They stood above her, flank to flank—wide, wet, eyelashy eyes and dished cow faces, waiting to see what she would do.

She went in to look at the baby. "Hey, pretty girl. What you doing?" she said.

She shook the crib for the baby. She pinched a piece of lint from its mouth.

"Mkgnao," she said. "Hulululu. Wakey, wakey, Baby."

The baby lay there. Rose picked it up, cupping its head the way she remembered seeing her sister do. She remembered the place where the bone had not met on the top of the baby's head, the dent you could press your thumb against and count the heartbeats through. She counted to twelve, or seven, and started to count again.

When they were five and six, the girls, when they were of an age for dolls, they loved the same blonde limbless thing until a day they fed it, set it to sit in the high chair where the girls themselves had used to sit, with the spoon they had learned to eat from.

When Rose pulled the doll's hair to bend back its neck to dribble ice cream into its mouth, the doll's eyeballs had dropped from their sockets and fallen into its head. It was something she had nearly forgotten.

Rose remembered, as a rule, very little:

A sheepdog drowned in the swimming pool in the year her hair was pixied.

She remembered her hair in a pixie.

She remembered a moose with removeable wounds, meaty pieces you could lift out and stick back in again.

Rose carried the baby out through the garden, feeling in her feet, her feet were bare, how the ground dipped and cooled in the beds, dampish where she had run the hose where she and Libby had dug up the iris.

She called, "Here, boy. C'mere, boy."

The dog came to her, smelling of sage, and walked along at her heels. They walked across the flagstone and over the shrivelled grass.

Where the grass stopped, the hogback began to slope away. At the foot of the slope were heaps of slag that grew, year by year, beside the concrete plant. A few lights went off in the concrete plant.

The baby fumbled at her, hungry.

"Are you hungry?" she said.

The dog whimpered.

"Not you," she said to the dog.

But the dog bucked and jumped at her feet to show that it was hungry. It trotted back to the house with its nose to the ground, looking for its bowl.

Rose pulled her robe across the baby. She started down over the hogback. Goatheads grew on the hogback, low along the ground. They had pale stems and narrow leaves you never saw until you walked into a patch of them, which is what Rose did. She tried walking first on the sides of her feet, where the skin was thick, and then on tip-toe. She tried stopping and standing on one foot to pull a few thorns from the other foot, feeling with her fingers for the thorns that had worked into the tenderest places. The baby cried, and the thorns on the foot Rose was standing on pushed in even deeper.

She went on. Behind her, a door squeaked open. The dog arrived with its bowl in its mouth and, picking its way among the thorns, walked along with her down the hill.

She was walking to a flat stone she remembered having sat on. The stone had been painted white, and the air around it looked lighter. It looked bigger, the stone, than it really was, as big to her as a smallish boat moored against the heaps of slag the chalky dust blew off of.

The dust was in her mouth, her eyes, she couldn't see quite. She saw the rim of the plains grow lighter, and the stone seemed to move away.

The dog dropped the bowl in the path they had walked and walked to the stone to watch her. She remembered the meat in her pocket. She had Big Bear's fork in her pocket.

"Watch me," she said to the dog. She walked into a patch of cactus, a cluster of pale, puffy crowns whose spines broke off in her arches.

She sang, "Baby, baby."

Her sister appeared in the light from the house and held her hands over the rim of the hill.

Rose took the baby's harness off, tossed it over her shoulder. She tossed the meat down the hill to the dog. Rose minced around in the cactus and then could not think what else to do.

The wind had begun to blow as it does when day begins in this part of the world. Her robe was flapping open. The baby was sucking at her, a bony, gummy mouth.

Libby called out.

Rose heard her. She could barely hear her.

She was thinking of the baby against her, how small she was and silky, and silky and creased and round.

She thought the baby would weep soon. It would look up and speak her name.

Rose found she was counting heartbeats. She was thinking she could feel her heart beat as you do sometimes in your finger-tips, behind your knees, in your teeth sometimes. She could feel that. But she could not keep up, counting—it was too fast, thready, the ragged, shallow, quickening pulse not of her own heart, she realized, but of the baby's heart, the dent on the top of the baby's head twitching against her arm. Her arm felt weak and tingly.

He came over the yard in his boxer shorts. He had hair all over his body.

Rose felt herself starting to pee, or bleed, she couldn't tell which. She saw him start down over the hogback and she squat-ted with the baby in the dust as he came. She felt the shudder he caused in the ground as he came, in her knees, in the bones of her hands—she swore that she could feel that—a blunt, heavy, bear of a man running down to her through the cactus, the goatheads, his wide flat feet winging out.

rooster, pollard, cricket, goose

We could do with him what we wanted. The old people left and left Goose here and what they left was ours.

They'd have taken him if they could. They took the glass from in the windows, they took the crib from the bend in the road. Our pa would have to drag a new crib out to keep the corncobs in. They took the cow in the wet field lowing. They took the blind pig beating the barn.

Down from the house where our ma stuck tight it went barn and barn and barn and crib and next the pond-bridge over the pond next the brocade couch in the pond where they had gone and dragged it. They left us the couch and the road paint sure from wherever cheap they had got it. They left the washer machine with its top torn loose down on its side beside the creek.

They took the knobs from the doors and the rods for towels and what bulbs that burned they could reach out to and loose them from their sockets. Anything much they could loose they took and everything they left behind we got to keep between us. I got the doll I saved from the johnnie that simpered when I hit it. I got the trees and the wind in the trees and the pond with the couch and the muskrat traps and the green gone garish on it. Pa got the horse and the hills.

The horse, we found between the barns where it had gone up and over. It had knocked its thick head on the road, Pa said. We were sitting in the truck.

We had checked the coop for chickens. We had seen that the crib was gone.

It went Pa then me then Ma in the truck with the baby asleep on her bosom.

They had hit it with a pipe, Pa said. Else it had gone up and over.

Ma got out like he told her to and went up the hill with the baby. I heard her high shoes on the road when she went and I heard when she stopped and rested.

The horse, I heard and would hear again the queer high birdish sound he made. It hung between the barns. He was laid out between the barns.

I got the barn and the hay in the barn and the dust coming slatted through the rafters. I got the pail for corn I beat to spook the rats from the crib when I fed when I came from the bus from school. It was my job to feed the animals, to fatten Maggie cow. I got the hay and the smell of the hay and the light snapping on on the barn.

The horse was Pa's and the hills he rode and the bees he dug that clouded him when he dragged the hooked plow with the tractor. The rabbits he dug he gave to me, I kept in the bowl in the washer machine thrown out where the creek ran through.

I stretched the come-along out like Pa told me. Because the others never did have a come-along to crank the horse over the gravel with to take him off on whatever it was they had brought to move away on. So they left him laid out on the hump of our road between the high walls of our barns.

The horse was dead, Pa said, or good as dead but what was the thin long sound he made, what were the lifting moons of his eyes when Pa came close with his gun? So he was good yet good for something.

A horse is worth something, easy, Pa said, you could sell him off handsome on the hoof in a blink. They would buy him from Pa by the pound. We could haul him up on the bed of Pa's truck, sell him off quick down the hill from us to pay for what they loosed from us the hooks and bulbs and sockets. And yet I thought to ride him. Yes. I thought to him: Hum up.

I looped the steel loop around his pastern first as quick in the dark as I could. I walked the slack out. I worked the handle some.

I saw the light go on in the house up the hill and then Ma in the window passing. So they left a light with the chairs all gone so Ma could see to sit the floor and hitch up her shirt for the baby. The baby always goes to the one so I ask who is the other one for. She laughs. You are as bad as your pa. Get on.

There are chickens to feed and cow Maggie. Two cobs twice for Maggie. There are board fences sure to creosote and thistle to dig from the fields when it bolts before the purple crowns. I muck the stalls and soap the tack and vet Pa's dogs they run the fields flushing birds all day. I am his girl Cricket. I climb the big oak on the hill Pa's hill even after when it is hit and burns and the burn blacks my skin my clothes.

I work the handle some and the slack is out and I can feel the horse start to pull over the hump of gravel. He lets his long high sound. Pa says it is like a goose so Goose but I never heard a goose as that, so long as that it warbled, not a sound like that and never since from bird nor horse nor man. Not even when Pa hit him.

He hit him in his head. Then was a sound a girl-girl lets, queerly sung and pretty. But that was some time after. That was when we shod.

First Pa thinks to work with him when he is up and well enough and we walk him down in the sun in the heat on the road between the barns. First Pa thinks to gentle Goose to ride him days we do not plow, afternoons we do not need to hoe nor pick nor harrow. Pa went to him first going easy talking sweetly in his ear. *Hope hope.*

He never did hit Goose at the first the night when Ma went off up the road. She went up the hill with the baby quick her hair a knot on her brightened head he reached for when she rested. First it was me Ma reached for. Then after me she rested. I took the strength she had, Pa said, so after me she rested.

Pa gets the hills and the oaks on the hills the old people called the farm by. Ma gets the house she climbs to, her shoes tapping bright on the road. Our ma gets the boy not yet a boy for Pa to need to work the fields while he is weak and small. She gets the way he smells the way he gums her how he coos.

Goose lets his long high sound. I feel him shudder across the gravel the ratchet clicking slow. I see him rest if I rest and flutter his nose but Ma will have something fixed for us and sits her chair to watch for us and sheets on the floor she has spread for us and the light is gone from the barn. They have loosed it from its socket hung from the spavined wall of the barn. *Get up.*

I taut the line some. I bring him easy.

I haul up the traps in the muck by and by from the bank where the old people left them. The dogs come to drink from the pond. They beat out a flattened path in the weeds in the burrs that

catch and mat my hair flown loose when first I found one. First
how we knew to look at all was once I heard Pa's dog. She had her
paw snapped up in the mouth of the trap in the gone-by weeds that
mark the pond in the rattling pods come winter. Summer coming
to its close. The fescue stiffly yellowed. And in the night Pa's dog
cries out from the drawn-back lip of the pond.

Be slow. Our Goose.

See the road slopes up. Take your time to calm you.

His breath comes weak and shallows. I let the line slack. He
throws himself to kneeling and his bones knock against the road.
He shoves his muzzle down on the road to rest so his thick head
saws above. Pa touches his flank with the gun. I ease up I think I
am easing up, the line gone slack to tap the road but I can never see
Goose quite. I can scarcely see him stand but to see the yellow of
his eye swing up and the white of his face against the road.

So he is up. I hear Pa humming to him slow and the coins in
his pants when he moves to him going, *Ho,* going, *Hope hope ho.*

Pa ought to have a sugar cube, a cigarette to give him.

He throws his head up. The stripe in his head when he
throws it streaks and see the dark will bleed it free, will from him
in the darkness wick the whiteness clean away. It is like our pa has
thrown it—how his bird dogs quake and trill.

You goose. First she called Pa so to tease him. But then Ma
called the baby *goose* and by and by each name for Pa I used to hear
her call him by she picked to name the baby with and mine I had
forgotten. Now we are only Pa to her and Pa and his girl Cricket.
Moving slowly in the road.

He throws his head up. It is like our pa has thrown it, gone
from the trees from the creek where he likes to work his dogs to the
field. Good dogs.

We can do with him what we want to. Sell him off quick on
the hoof if we like to grind his bones to give the dogs the inly tubes
and organs keep them fed and fit and strong. They are field dogs,

bird dogs all. Pa throws them the wing of the cut-away goose in the falling dark and the dogs at his feet and they stay they stay, the wing dipping down until he moves his hand to school them.

And then his long high sound. And so Pa named him Goose for the goose for the wing he throws his dogs.

Goose lunges at Pa so much as he can but I have got him looped up still, Pa tripping back with his gun at his chest so I ratchet the line to hold him. I cannot hold Pa. Only watch him slowly falling. He takes a long time falling.

Pa's dogs bed down and whinge. *You quit.* But they are thinking what will happen what is next to come?

Time comes Pa thinks to ride him. Out between the barns. He rides to the oaks the lightning hits along the fence cow Maggie rubs to leaning while she fattens. Past the coop the chickens pecking slowly at their corn. Past Pa's prize yellow rooster learned to blind his favored hens.

Pa's dogs, they are bird dogs all—but are they bird enough to guess at him? At Pa's prize yellow rooster? Who appeared in a fluff in the barn—the day Goose rode Pa past and every day thereafter. And sat his back thereafter. Who flew his coop to bide his days sitting Goose's withers—could they guess at such as him?

And at the day we shod him?

And of the bees Pa plowed?

I am not one to picture it not nearly even half of it not Ma in her chair past autumn not the wrangled plow. Nor Goose. The rooster shyly by him. Pa's. And then the rooster Goose's. Only walking back to rooster pecking gently at his hens.

Nor that. I had not pictured that. And not the picked-over eyes of the hens bright as the yolks of the eggs we take left seeping in their feathers.

Not the blood the baby lets not the milk the baby lets, Ma's shirt run pinkly through. Nor that. Him plumping at her bosom.

Time was I was Ma's. Nor that. Nor time was Pa was also.

Not Pa when I come upon him. He has dragged across the pond.

I am not cut to picture. To stand at the bank and puzzle out I am cut to cut and run.

The gun fires when he wallops the road. Then Goose is up and hanging.

The old people have come. I thought Goose had seen the old people come rolling home to claim him.

And so he hung there. What to do.

I touched the line once. They couldn't loose him. They could go on back from wherever they'd come and forget they ever saw him stood and pawing where they left him in a heap upon the road.

They could find another. There are others after Goose. There are Mouse and Pepper, Blue, Prim Sue and Candysara. Cribbing at the barn.

I tie Pa's bootstrings every morning. Did his bootstrings loose I tied for him did his pantlegs make him fall?

Ma takes one pair and me another. We hem the legs on Pa's short side from the time when Pa was a boy my size and crumpled in his bed. *Get up.* And Pa could not get up and not. And not for a long time after. So is it mine or Ma's dread cross? Who take one pair and one another. We are not much with our needles. And Pa is fallen across the road.

He seems to quit there. He seems to quit and stiffen, ready for the blow.

Goose would throw himself off from us. He would fly himself over the barn he thought come soft on his hooves in the field where he grazed with we two dumbly watching.

Then he was over. Goose flung himself on over. I heard his bones, the clatter and snap, his head a rind against the road bursted wetly open. He lay there—his legs sprung stiff, his corded neck—his body hauled in chinked from stone to mark the field the fallen dead the bloody day forgotten.

Pa softly now, "Let up."

I held the line taut. I saw I held the line taut still from the coil where I let it.

The nightsky stooped and held its breath, the trees bent too to listen—for the sputter and tick the quieting tide of Goose's reedy pipes and valves the rocking iridescent humps and hollows of his organs.

And Pa again, "Let up." Still I heard *Get.*

Pa struggled up from where he fell and knocked the grit from his pants I stitched, the sloppy hem, and he nodded. Pa came at me with his hand high up. He had never hit me yet but still I stood to let him.

The line had cut some through. I had looped it over the curl of fur above the hoof you sell them on and it had dug some through. His eye had spun wide up in the dark to regard the stars above. The moon on its slow crossing.

His burblings—mine—my cross to bear, my thin bitten birdish shrill he let, my name though Pa had thought it—*Goose. Goose* and also *Cricket.* We were named for the sounds thrown from us yes for a dream's long soured tongue.

And so I loosed it. I shook the line some. Nothing not a twitch not a nostril flared no breath no lifting brisket. So I could do it easy ease the loop the cable from his pastern where I cut him. I felt the heat rise from him. I felt the give in my knees when I kneeled by him and the heat of the softened road. So we could winch him up now. He had made it easy. We would wait for the light for the morning.

Morning. Hello, little farm.

Still we wake to him up come sunup. We are sleeping all on the sheet Ma spread and Goose is scrolloping over the road.

I snip Pa's toenails for him turn his hem and tie his boots who cannot reach to do it.

I can smell the barn. I smell in my hair the baby too he gummed it as we rode.

Pa clips the leadshank on him. He feels along his bones.

Pa leads him off between the trees me and Ma standing out in our gowns she wears to walk in time the fallen dew the hill we climb to reach her. I sit the chair her chair to watch her, watch the nightshade fill behind her see the bats loop briefly through. Her small boy nearby sleeping.

At length when once the snow has come to keep us snugly home, Ma goes sunup to nightfall gowned else sits the bath from meal to meal the latch thrown once the baby walks to keep him always with her to keep him safely in.

She has heard us at our chores by then. We have backed Goose onto the slab by then. The rooster crowing on.

Pa's dogs spooked about for the moons Pa clipped, for the tailings curled from his hooves filed flat to take the shoe and he cussed them. Cussed his horse his dogs. His girl with the mangled paw stumping in who sat with me at his knees should he sit should he think to nudge her head. Let her bump her ribs against him.

After her I found the others easy. You go by your nose through the weeds for the traps going low to the ground like a dog. Red fox I found and muskrat, coon and the paw of what I do not know in the muck cow Maggie made of the banks of the pond I would wade in the dry out into.

The old people could have found them caught in the dry time when they moved. Then I would not have had to. Would not have had to smell them then nor burr my hair to get to them nor haul them onto the bridge for Pa so Pa could see to flay or gut or what any else he did to them or sort the parts to bury.

We buried them back by the chicken coop in sight of the pond where they swam if they swam or only came and drank from. Soon the rooster flapped over the pond—his Goose had gone from the field. The rooster come to sit Goose's back flapped in his grief to the couch when Goose passed come rain come sleet come snow. Crowing on.

His hens in the coop to hear him. I lay in my bed and heard him, the moon sweeping past, the stars.

Cricket you Cricket you.

See the white of his face swung up?

His bright eye webbed and curdled?

And then when we had blinded him and set him out in the field to browse I saw the skin seal and crumple saw in the cold it was blent and gathered.

They will do it to a baby too a rooster will give him half a chance he does it to his own. And his hens' eyes are small.

I lay in my bed and pictured it.

Pictured Pa when I came upon him.

I came upon him in the wet months yet the flying leaves the sinking grass the geese dropped from their wedges yet and scudding across the pond.

I had come on the bus from school. I skipped. I swung my feet through the fallen leaves to smell the sweet wet smell of them to smell the wind the needling rain that in the night had felled them. The leaves flew up and clung to me to the ratty flounce of the skirt I wore the bitten ridge of my shinbones. I stopped at the pond to peel them from me.

I could hear the tractor then. You turn the fields to fallow them. I liked to listen for Pa to know where he might leave the harrowbed the plow.

I heard him. But I did not think *Pa* at first I did not think *listen.* I sang my song the coming home song against his note I had not heard and hope again to never. Still I looked about and saw him. He was wallowed up on the couch in the green with the yellow bead the pond was deep on the couchback scarcely showing.

He could not be Pa. He was something in the wet the old people left that had loosed itself from the muck as it went and yet it spit my name. With still our barns to pass between, the hill to the house to run. I ran. I ran the day the bees got Pa and ran the day I held his Goose in the washroom where we shod. But I did not run far. I heard him bellow. You try it try to run. Drop to your hands if the grass is high and dream he cannot find you there with your heart knotted small as the rabbits new-born he brings to you in the crown of his hat the days he plows to calm. But I have never saved one. I have never saved one yet of all the ones he brings to me I have lost them all.

I lay on the bank and watched him. The longer I kept away from Pa the harder it was to go to him.

And yet I went to him. I knocked the bees from his neck for him Pa gone in his hurt not hearing me not a place on him to hold him by I held him by his hair. Through the green I swam him. I could have walked the pond but it took my shoes from my feet the silken bottom. Me and Pa dragged a stripe in the green where I swam where it folded against Pa's head. Pa Pa.

Once we grew a pig so fat even its eyelids fattened, ear and jowl and bursting cheek and by and by its eyeballs—squeezed— stood away loose from its head.

Then Pa. Bellowing out of the wallow. The cow to her teats to cool. The tractor run up on a stump and stopped and still at its ticking idle. I made my hands a stirrup—Pa's legs were too swelled to bend. *Swing up.* And from the time of riding shotgun years I knew which stick to muscle, which to back to raise the plow when once we had it scraping up loud against the road.

Ma in her chair past autumn. Us come up come dew come snow. The baby let to his knees at the screen to scream the day the bees swarmed Pa and Ma came out to swat at us going *Gracious lord above.*

Think back to when time was in her—my soft head broken

through. Before that. When time was she was Pa's. Before my hair I grew in her that made her retch and swoon.

A girl. And her boy sick and small. I took the strength she had in her. I kept them up nights nights in her: their Cricket. Chirruping in the swill.

Boy, her boy, her funny runt. He could not be Pa's. Who came before they thought his name and stayed they had not thought he might for such a long time after. *Boy*, she called him. *Goose, you goose,* and *mister*—Ma thinking not to choose a name to have to have to call him by should he be taken from her.

We never took him from her. Even when he crawled. Nor say I ever came to her to cut my name most fine in her not before nor after Ma swelling as he grew.

I was all Pa's girl. The barns were mine and the hay in the barns and Pa and the trees and the cows. Cow Maggie leaned against me. The birds flew south by the stars. Barn and barn and barn and pond the road climbing out through the fields. Mine and Pa's, my pa's. The high quiet wobbledy stars. And Ma where she sat in the window was ours and sat in the shut-away buttery gold, the dogs at our heels the stars. Should you wish.

Ma's shirt bled pinkly through.

The seed-blown fields the wickerings. The slickened births and murders, ours, the fierce wide blowing day.

I tended to him gently. Pa wallowing in the tub. He would swell to fit it. And swell till he could not budge from it and I would spoon a mash to him and keep the water cooled for him and nest his head in my pillow. His eye unloosed like a doll's. Fetch a sledge. Break him duly from it.

Pa's arms puffed out to float from him and seep in milky puddles, his skin so hot to touch it scalds. I did not touch it. I worked the coughing spigot, churned the cold to sap the heat slowly not to hurt him. And made as not to hear him his voice not his no voice at all—a green sea grief a great whale culled and keening in its traces.

I daubed a paste where he was stung a curdly dull against his skin I first swiped bright with butter. Pa. Who plowed the bees it comes to me to see if Ma would see to him to see if she would tend to him but Ma would not have come.

Why seem at last to hear him? Ma would not have come.

And who was it came upon him?

And so I took it slow. I made Ma's clucks and muddlings and swabbed and slowly doctored him. I had no Goose to think of no price to fetch no mouths to fill no deed to hide the doing of.

No day yet when we shod.

It's me Pa Pa it's Cricket.

Get.

I was not her. Not Ma and never Cricket quite but proof she had not come.

I took to sleeping in the barn else the sinking grass in the leaves unhinged in the wind. Pa's rooster nightly crowing.

Pa when he was up again and shrunk into himself again rode Goose unshod through our honeyed woods our creeks our windfall autumn. Among the lowly creatures named and ours to daily tend. We are sloppy in our tending. Our swallows catch in the raftered dark our rabbits are turned from the fields. Fox we trap and whistle pig and the spotty domes of our turtles crush in the wet upon our road. And in our hay we gather. And too the narrow fellows sunning lazy in the stubble catch—snakes pressed between the flakes of hay as though we mean to keep them, and faith by them in the shut-away days the snowbound weeks we wait to breathe that the fields are strewn and rooted through with bees with bodies sleeping.

Pa wore Goose away his hooves split and curled and then a day I came from school Pa brought him to me saddled and swung me up to ride him. Pa gave me a whip to run him with. Goose could not walk it looked to me he seemed to wince to stand there.

Up the hill I ran him.

We ran until Pa could not see and then we let him come to us come gimping up the hill to us to snap the lunge line on. Pa swung me up again. So he could run us. So we might see she watched him run us. He stood at the hub of the circle we ran in whatever dusk was left to us and Ma appeared in the windowlight in her sorry robe. *Hup ho.*

The night closed in the early cold. Goose beneath me frothed and steamed and still my hands my skinny arms grew thick to me and shook. My bare legs burned beneath my skirt against the sweating saddleflaps and so I tried to hold them off so that when Goose tripped he threw me, he would throw me, I would fly through the trees like a doll. Soon enough.

Quick the snow the brittling cold. As quick the thaw comes on.

I trick Goose into the trailer then his blinkers on to calm him and grain in the bin to steady him after we have beat at him and cussed and poked and whooped at him till Pa has gone off for his gun.

After the day we shod this was. After the snow the thaw had come.

No bird for us no Christmas.

The snow slumping against the barn. "You load the cur before I'm back else I am going to have to—"

To have to. Pa could do with him what he wanted—he was toddling off for his gun. I did not try to stop him but to think to walk Goose in.

Ma gone from her chair the tent jerked down we had hung at the hearth to snug in. Yet we were not what kept her. It was not in us to keep her.

And so I walked him in.

The first I saw I ran from him. I did not think *Pa* at first but is it dead or living.

This was before we blinded Goose before the time we trailered him our Ma going off with her wheelbarrow her boy in a bunch in the wheelbarrow how small against the road.

Before any of that. Before we shod this was. Before the rooster flapped onto the pond.

And yet I ran from Pa. Crept back. Before the bees died off I did. Before the fescue yellowed. I lay on the bank to look at him. The pods of the milkweed swelled and split and the seed by its silken feathery plumes as it was meant to do broke away.

And then we shod him.

The day was dull the day we shod him and cold before the snow had come and Pa sent me out to fetch Goose out of the withering grass where he browsed. I walked through the gate with my pail at my knees and called to him over the field.

He came to me.

He let me come to him, whinnying, that day as any other.

The days were dry then. The corn a stubble. The apples blew into the fields, a glut that year—I could find him. It was easy enough to find Goose—he was feasting beneath the trees. He quit to look at me. Pa's rooster pecking lazily a drubbing on his withers.

Pa had fired the forge in the barn the barn dark to me but for the embers there the shadows rayed and flinching the cottony raftered dark. Goose was shy of it, I brought him gently in, he was skittish.

I backed him into the washroom into the crossties where we shod. I leaned my chest, a boy's, against him. I felt my heart at the bone in his head his breath the wet of the grass he ate and sweet against my belly. *Hush.*

I kept it to me.

At the first even Pa was kind. He clipped away where the hoof began at the end to hook and tear. He kicked the shards the cutaway moons to his dogs to take to nibble at at the end of the barn and hide. He rasped the hoof flat, he picked a small stone from the frog.

The shoe nested in the forge on the fire—outside, winter's early winded dark advancing slowly on.

The rooster stood to crow for it. That day as any other. But Pa when the rooster crowed jerked up and let his hollowed sound he made the day I came upon him swarmed. He jabbed Goose in his brisket. Goose already lunging. Pa gone to his knees on the slab.

The rooster flapped to the rafters. The sparrows swept from the barn.

He filed the hoof flat. You have to rasp it flat to take the shoe to ride the wash and hillside slopes to pass the house and Ma in the house to pass the coop the chickens.

He pinched the shoe from the forge—it was flaring, a shaking liquid yellow. He hooked the shoe over the anvil then over the battered nose—you have to turn it. Pound it to make a fit of it bore the slim squared holes.

I knew Pa's knees were swelling—I had heard them knock against the slab. His long face pinched and fallowed, I saw, who saw ahead as I knew he must the bruisy syrupy blue of skin the selvage pressed of the pants I hemmed sloppily upon it. I would have to cut Pa's pants from him—from the burl the knotted sickened joint and ice or lance or sit to bend or what any else Pa thought to show he could bully through the doing of and so we two kept on with it so we two said nothing.

He punched the nail through—once, three times again, on the one shank and then on the other. To keep the shoe fast. To drive the nails through—square and blunted. Eight in all. I knew the sound and counted.

Pa held the shoe against his hoof. The shoe was hot still it was hissing and the stink of hide of hair or hoof the twangy burning smell rose up and Goose threw himself against me. Pa held him. He did what he could to hold him Pa he kept him wedged against the wall we hang the tack the leadshanks on the picks and forks and shovels.

Tell her that.

He tapped the nail in.

Tell your ma I tried to calm him. That at the last we twitched him. To make it easy. I meant to calm him. I put myself between you tried to keep you safe from harm. No harm meant. You could not trust him. He was game but you could not trust him. He would throw you into the trees he would he would drag you across the fields.

I let Pa twitch him. So I could hold him. So the day might come I thought so of the weeks I sulked to school.

Pa drew out Goose's lip where the stripe blazed through the velvet soft that veered across and snatched down the twitch the silver bars upon it hard and twisted. It was easier then to hold Goose shaking quiet on the slab. I drew his head down slowly and pressed my face to the white of his face how soft where the stripe swept through.

Pa tapped a nail in. He went hoof to hoof in the graying light. *How quick the dark came on. Tell her that.*

But I could not yet think of Ma of what we would need or not to tell but thought of the day I would ride our Goose in my boots to school. I would tie Goose off on the chalky racks the city kids lash their bicycles to, would come to him between the bells to curry him to feed him.

Hey horsie girl.

Of course they teased me. Would. Who wished to be me.

How I pressed my heart to his brisket.

Pa wedged each hoof between his knees his shoulder thrown against Goose hard to keep him tipped against the wall we hang the leads and halters on the shoe for luck to hold him. I felt his breath against my chest a wind drawn rough across my throat and felt the cool the whips of spit the snot swept down from his nostrils yes and of his mouth the velvet there where the stripe blazed through.

You get. And the rooster too. *Get get.*

I kept the loop of his mouth pinched fast the twist in the loop that made him wheeze that Pa had stopped to show to me that made him drip and gurgle. And still I could not hold him. I was sick in myself to hold him so so Pa could shove and cuss at him so Pa could treat him roughly.

He swung the rasp back.

It would not be long.

We would leave our tools and the cooling forge and make our way up from the barn. Soon enough.

Then I could cut Pa's pants from him. Who cannot reach to do it. Who have not kept him from it. The selvage dug well in.

Pa kept on as I knew he must who knew by him the way of things who knew to watch him swing his rasp he swung at Goose's head his knees enough to think *he's mine. He is mine he is mine he is mine.*

Will be.

I will cook and clean for him and sew and scrub his feet for him and shine his boots and buckles.

Keep him safe from harm.

Say that.

That it was easy, it would have been easy—to lose an eye on the wash-room wall on the hooks and nails we hang tack from he could do it to himself tell her he could do it easy.

That he is fractious. He is meant to be worked and strong tell her. How quick the dark came on.

It came on.

Pa beat at Goose about the knees the rasp struck in behind and hard where you can hear the bones in him where you can make him buckle.

I would not have pictured it—that you could make him buckle. That Pa could fell him in the crossties hanging ready for the blow.

Goose dropped to his knees his rump yet high as if to let me throw my foot my leg across and ride him. My hat flying up to school. *Wheeo.*

He quit there—to let before Pa came at him his last breath ratchet through. And then Pa came at him.

I thought how the white swept up. Pa fallen across the road. *Wheeo.*

Because Pa could not have rolled from him. Pa could not have moved.

He swung the rasp back. He brought it hard across his head his rolling curdled eye I saw.

Cricket you Cricket you.

Quick a girl's sweet wurbled note. Quick as that the wet-tish thuck the jellied seep of his eyeball burst the flies the puss like honey.

We set him out then. When it was done then. I walked Goose out on his blinded side and set him loose like Pa had said back in the back and hidden field the deer came to to lie in. We walked up the hill and washed our hands and sat and ate our supper.

She had fried three eggs for supper for us as Ma had come those weeks to do no matter what Pa said of it and three again come morning. And Pa said nothing of it and not again when light had come and Ma went out with her boy in the snow that as we slept flew down. Her tracks went out to the fence I sat the days Goose ran the sloping field and turned toward the barn and quit there well shy of the bend in the road.

She came back then. I put my mind to it—to the tracks I had to go by. There were two of them going she left in the snow and not a step she came back by.

She had gone away twice down the hill, I thought. She had gone away once the mother we knew who sat for us in the window. Then look on her heels came the other. Here came the one from before the boy we had forgotten was hers to ever be or ever was ours to know.

I liked to think of it—that she could walk herself out away from us from what we did or did not do she could call herself out on the road going out going out in her boots in the unbroken snow that we would know at the last we had lost her.

And yet the tracks quit.

She would find Goose in the barn she thought. She would see him she thought from the bend in the road see what we had done to him who sat at her table after and ate the meal she cooked for us and slept in the beds she made for us and so she quit well shy of it and came away back to home. She walked herself back up the hill to us walking backward her back to the wind to keep her boy from the snow.

The snow climbed in the trees in the fences. A night would pass a morningtime and soon Pa would set upon her again and break what eggs I brought to her that the hens before the rooster quit still had in them for laying. After that I did not bring the eggs. After that they did not lay them.

The rooster went from the field and back to sit the broken

back of the couch stood up in the ice of the pond. No thought in his head to rooster. No eggs to bring for Pa to break for Ma to fry for supper then even should we want some.

I thought I would not want some. I would break an egg in his socket I thought let the yolk freeze bright and round. Should Goose lie down.

And then he lay down—the night of the day the wind came warm and the thaw set in the sudden melt and the birds appeared and bickered and swerved in the steam twisting up from our farm.

We hitched the trailer then. That we might use him. Sell him off quick on the hoof down the hill in the warm while we could move.

I had kept Goose's tail in a braid for him and kept his head in a hood for him so the wind could not eat at the socket. The last of our sorry apples dropped I had kicked to him in the field where he lies where he pawed at the snow for what grass there was and picked the leaves he could get to yet from the beech the oak the whippy trees at the edge of the woods that held them. What he did not eat the deer took to and to the cobs of corn I brought and his coat grew thick and ratted in the wind and his hipbones stood out from him.

We kept our heads down. The cold had deepened. I tramped a path past the coop the failing hens the rooster would not when the cold had come leave the pond to rooster.

I thought at first he would ride with me out in the pail with the corn to the field. And so I stopped at the bank to cluck at him. He turned his tail to me. I brought his prize hens to the bank to see and scratch to spread to tempt him. Before the pond was skinned with ice I ferried him back through the muck the weeks yet never once did I see him eat nor seem to think to rooster, never once did I pass the crib to climb the hill to the house to Ma but that he hadn't flapped back out to the couch to announce what we had done.

This was when the freeze augered in, this was in the thaw.

In the thaw of the year when the water rose Pa's bird seemed to walk upon it.

I went the while before the thaw before the hillsides snicked and steamed and then the once thereafter after Ma had gone. I knew to call to him, picking my way once the creek froze through between the spindly boles of trees the needled limbs of the buckthorn there where yet the small dark berries clung the beads in rimpled clusters. I shook in my pail as I went to him the corn I was not to bring to him. I brought cigarettes and sugar cubes crumbling apart in my pockets.

Hope hey. Hope hey. I meant to tend to him, to swab and slowly doctor him. To sweep my thumb through his socket. A day came I came upon Goose there forgetting myself to speak to him and stood upon his blinded side and he swung away and kicked me. I let him kick me.

Then it was easy. Then I could quit then.

The field was hidden. I tossed my pail back to the back of the crib and the rats there shied and scuttled out and trotted away to the barn.

So it was easy. The cold had deepened.

I went the once Pa sent me out when the thaw set in to fetch him. I saw his head rise up to see me. Otherwise I went no more.

We snugged in when the worst of the cold had come and fashioned a room with the blankets we had with the tablecloths Ma kept to spread should a guest appear should Christmas. I rode Pa's back to drive the nails to stand in his hands in the stirrups he made and hit at the few ruined crooked nubs the old people left to hang the walls. We brought our sheets our pillows in and ate and slept in what warmth there was from the fire we nursed and prodded. Ma ripening in her gown. Our shadows should we sit in quiet there yet flinching against the walls.

Ma kept her eye fast on her boy. Sitting her silk chair.

"Time was I thought the milk teeth came to make the women stop it," Pa said. "Let them rest a time—for the next to breed. Give a man his chance abed. Time was."

She set the baby down on his feet at her feet. Should he squall she swung him up again.

"But it makes your ma keep at it, same with that boy as you."

Her boy. Him lolling yet at her bosom.

We woke for weeks to snowfall the curling drifts the wind banked up to pin our flapping door. The hedge disappeared the leeward fence cow Maggie walked out over to find her way to the barn. No school for weeks no place we went our tractor left with the broken plow on the road where Pa sprung off from it come up on him and over until all but the lip of the highside tire the wind picked clean seemed gone.

Then of a night a velvet wind and foreign swept our farm.

Pa legged me over the windowsill. He heaved me out in my mucklucks onto the slope of snow. The slabs of snow of thickened ice already in the pooling glare crept across the rooftops. I took my list to go by: cigarettes sardines D-con cheese.

Barn and barn and crib and pond and on the pond Pa's rooster—spun—our grudging weathervane. I think he thought to crow at me who never crowed by morninglight and so I waved my cap at him and waved as I went at his baffled hens, sunk to my peep in the snow.

"How you?"

They had lights at the store and the woodstove burned and the wind flown hard in the blackened pipe sucked and moaned and tumbled. I gathered my goods and bagged them. The girl held out her hand for the money she knew my pa would never send me with and quick I turned for home from her the thaw sunk deep upon us.

Every stone and matted leaf and fence and sloping fallow steamed. The ice on the pond broke soft when I passed and soft the newts the spotty frogs the dull fish frozen in. The barn the mossy pond I smelled and in the wind the flowers bloomed where it had crossed to reach us. It came on.

Ma went back in her blotted gown to the back of the house she had happened from and found her hat her dungarees her chalky split galoshes. So quick I went to fetch Goose. He lay in the field on his blinded side in a patch pawed free of snow.

I let him stop for a time for the apples that dropped and palmed him the last of the treats I had kept the months for him in my pockets.

We took the path past the crib. I knew no other way to go so as not to pass her. She would go on. She had her bag at her knee her hat on. Her boy in a bunch in the wheelbarrow.

I led him along his hood pulled free him lathered in the sudden warm his brisket gaunt and heaving. *Cricket you Cricket you.*

It would not be long. I knew as much to look at Ma her flicks and starts and sudden flush her voice like something burst in her should she gap her mouth to use it.

I went on. I led him up between the barns where Pa had drawn the trailer up and stood the high gates open.

Ma turned back the once and once again to bring herself to go. We stood on the road and watched her. The road black in the wet in the sudden thaw in the steam that dipped and gathered grown so thick to squat upon our pond that it seemed not our rooster there but the air itself yet crowing.

Stay. Stay. So go.

I gave Goose his head to lunge at Pa to beat the air to strike at him should Pa swing past where Goose could see else think to speak or touch him. To see if she would tend to him. But Ma was going on.

She went up through the lopped and pollarded trees I kept as she went a count of. Pa's dogs at her heels since the barn. Good dogs.

I leant against Pa's legs with them. I licked his pants when I was small with them with him not looking. Quick.

You get.

Pa toddling off for his gun.

Goose scraped at the road the piddling stream with the shoe those months he had not thrown that I would pry for luck from him and clip the braid of his tail from him hung fat with the mud we had hauled him through, the slickened clay and loamy sweet, and thinking I would go there yet where Goose yet lay in the sun and moon I found a tree a buckthorn near and deep against it hung them.

I blinkered him to calm him.

I walked on in ahead of him and we could hear Pa coming back, I was backed against the trough with him wedged away under the bars from him and Pa had creaked the swing-gate shut and Goose went back to thrashing. I felt my head flung back. Pa stood up on the running board and the shaft of the gun pushed through.

So it was Pa shot him.

It is for my sake Pa shot him.

I was in the stall beside him and the trailer shook and ringing quit and the blood of my face where Goose opened it ran free in my mouth and warm.

Enough for me. *No matter.*

Ma looked back the once and went on.

All that she had left to us and what is yet to come to us the oaks on the hill the lightning hits the fox in the field in the weeds

I keep gone red to gray come autumn—it is enough for me. *No matter.*

I will sing Pa her song the getting up song she sang to me in the morningtime when she leaned to me to nudge me and the baby was in her hair.

I could smell him from her hair.

I slip through the muck the gone-by weeds the flatted grass the dogs bend down and think *if I could run from him* else think *I never came on him wallowed up on the couch in the green suppose Cricket supposing.*

We sat on the shore and watched him.

I did not know in myself what to do for Pa nor what there might be in tending him to call so even gently. To say: I tend him gently.

Pa would have me poke at him. He would have me pinch and twist at him.

Yet to say: *I tend him gently.* And ever in the dusk in the sinking light I knead his feet his withered legs to move the gout and feed him.

Am I not his girl Cricket?

Enough for me. No matter.

I sing Ma's song to him.

Our blessings count.

Enough for me to keep our Goose and in myself the truth of him and the dogs grow fat and eat of him and by the silken sweet of glue we spread across our palms to peel the skin I feel him with me and feel of the seeds that split in me and of the living harvest, shell and hide and cloven tongue and of the fruit and fowl we strew the yolky eyes the deer we cull the great whales flensed for blubber.

Ever so. Ever so gently.

I lie in the field and picture it. Who have come to be one to picture it. How long it was Goose hung there. Such a time it was he hung there pawing softly at the stars.